Professor Hayes

Andrew Jackson Hayes, immediately dubbed 'Professor Hayes', is hired to serve as San Juan, New Mexico's first male teacher. In short order he upsets the community's most stodgy matrons when he marries Rachel – a woman recently arrived on a marriage train – demonstrates his pistol skills, brawls and frequents the saloon.

Fired, Hayes and Rachel move to a high valley owned by the professor. They and some of their nearest neighbours whom they befriend, come under a series of attacks by unknown aggressors, attacks they suspect are related to gold on their land.

Can Hayes and his allies survive intermittent skirmishes with Apache warriors, as well the multiple attacks from aggressors whose identities remain a mystery. . . ?

By the same author

The Staked Plains

Professor Hayes

Billy Moore

A Black Horse Western

ROBERT HALE · LONDON

© Billy Moore 2014
First published in Great Britain 2014

ISBN 978-0-7198-1331-3

Robert Hale Limited
Clerkenwell House
Clerkenwell Green
London EC1R 0HT

www.halebooks.com

The right of Billy Moore to be identified as
author of this work has been asserted by him
in accordance with the Copyright, Designs and
Patents Act 1988

Typeset by
Derek Doyle & Associates, Shaw Heath
Printed and bound in Great Britain by
CPI Antony Rowe, Chippenham and Eastbourne

CHAPTER ONE

Every conversation stopped and every eye turned toward the long-legged black horse and its rider coming up the one dusty street of San Juan, New Mexico. People adjusted their hat brims and turned their heads, looking for a way to block the bright mid-morning sun against which the horse and rider appeared in vague outline.

The horse drew more attention than the rider; it stood more than sixteen hands and was soot-black, but it was the smooth gait of a southern plantation walking horse rather than its appearance that really riveted the attention. Such horses, bred for riding comfort rather than speed or quickness, were rare in New Mexico, where most people preferred the hardy mustang stock.

When the false front of Gibson's Mercantile blocked the sun so that the people could see the horse more clearly, they saw a thin horse, the bones of its withers and rump clearly visible. Horsemen in the crowd, though, noted that the horse was thin from hard work rather than lack of feed or care. What the horsemen noticed instead were bright clear eyes, a smooth shiny coat, neatly trimmed hoofs with new shoes and an alert demeanor.

In contrast, only the rider's clothing would attract attention to him. He would stand no more than five feet, six inches and appeared slight of build. His black suit, white shirt, and black tie weren't so unusual for a big day like the Fourth of July, but the suit was spotless and neatly pressed, the boiled white shirt crisply starched, his face smoothly shaved, and the hat flawless. The contrast between the rider's immaculate appearance and the hard-used appearance of the horse wasn't lost upon the watchers.

The man rode directly to the table set up on the rough new planks of the sidewalk in front of Gibson's Mercantile. A sign, neatly lettered in the same blue paint and white trim as the signs that identified the San Juan Bank and, next door, Gibson's Mercantile, announced: 'Noon, Fourth of July, 1868 One Mile Race: $10 Entry, $100 Prize.'

Most of the townspeople didn't recognize the rider as the new schoolteacher, who most had seen only once weeks earlier, until they noticed the manner in which he slightly dragged his left leg as he walked. Andrew Jackson Hayes – the townspeople had already begun to refer to him as Professor Hayes – took a moment to adjust his hat before he strode to the table set up to register entrants into the big horse race.

Wisps of smoke from the fire over which quarters of beef sputtered drifted over the knot of people hanging around the registration table. The odor of beef and smoke mixed with the odor of the boards of the sidewalk, so recently cut that resin still seeped to the surface.

A smiling man in casual denim work pants and a blue plaid shirt stood as Professor Hayes approached. The difference in the two men was startling. The man at the table towered over Hayes by almost a foot and was so well proportioned that one only noticed how massive he was in comparison to others nearby. The skin of his face and hands was surprisingly tan for one with such light blonde hair and blue eyes. He extended his hand toward Hayes.

'Professor Hayes,' he said, 'you might not remember me. I'm Devlon Gibson.'

Hayes smiled at the idea that anyone might forget Devlon Gibson and responded, 'Of course, Mr Gibson.' Gibson's hand dwarfed that of Hayes. 'Is it too late to enter the race?'

'No,' Gibson responded, surprise evident on his face. 'But you don't intend to enter, do you?'

'Is there any reason why I shouldn't?' Professor Hayes asked. His startlingly light gray eyes, made to look even lighter against his black hair and the deeply browned skin of his hands and face, locked with those of Devlon Gibson.

'I guess not, Professor,' Gibson said. He paused to take in the expressions of other townspeople. 'There is wagering, you realize?'

'Good,' Hayes said, and laid a ten dollar gold piece on the table. 'And do I understand correctly that you offer two-to-one odds versus your horse in side bets?'

Gibson's eyes drifted toward the walking horse Hayes had left standing in the street. The horse's eyes followed Hayes' every movement. As Gibson's eyes met with several in the crowd, a smile crept across his face as if sharing some private joke. 'This is only a one mile race. Are you sure you want to run your horse in it?'

Hayes smiled slightly as he pulled a small leather poke from a pocket inside his coat. 'If you have scales, I believe this is one hundred dollars worth of gold.' Hayes opened the poke and spilled small, rough kernels of gold on to the paper that listed race participants.

Gibson's eyes glanced from the gold to the professor and quickly back to the gold. The big man recovered his aplomb, quickly swept the gold back into the leather bag, and dropped it into a metal box. 'Certainly, I'll cover your wager, Professor. It just caught me by surprise, you being a teacher and all.'

Bystanders smiled. Several poked their neighbors in the side with their elbows.

'But to be neighborly and welcome you to San Juan, I'll offer you three to one. Three hundred dollars if you beat my horse,' Gibson offered.

'Quite generous of you, Mr Gibson,' Hayes responded. He started to turn toward his horse, but Gibson's voice stopped him.

'I'll also put the title of my racing mare against that black walking horse.'

Hayes nodded and offered his hand.

'What do you call that long-legged black horse, Professor?' someone in the crowd asked.

'I call him Napoleon,' Professor Hayes answered, quiet good humor in his voice.

'Why Napoleon?' a red-faced farmer asked.

'Because you can see all the bony parts,' Hayes answered and smiled.

Laughter rippled through the crowd as the teacher walked away. Word quickly spread that Professor Hayes had bet one hundred dollars on his skinny walking horse in a one mile race. Most thought betting on a walking horse in a short race was funny, although a few scolded Gibson, telling him that he should feel ashamed for taking the new teacher's money. A hundred dollars was several months' salary for the teacher, not to mention that it would set him afoot.

The big black horse followed without Hayes touching his reins. The crowd scattered from in front of Gibson's Mercantile. A tall, older man with long white hair sat in a wooden rocking chair with his long legs stretched casually in front of him and sipped from a glass of whiskey. 'Your money just turned to water, Devlon,' he drawled.

Gibson looked at Doc Ramsey in surprise. 'You don't think that walking horse can compete with my mare, do you?' he asked.

Doc Ramsey pulled five golden eagles from his pocket. 'On the professor's horse,' he offered.

'Same three to one for you, Doc.' Gibson grinned but underneath he couldn't help but wonder. The old rascal did know horses. But his mare had never been beaten, Gibson reassured himself.

CHAPTER TWO

By ten minutes until noon, several hundred people – everyone from San Juan plus a healthy sprinkling of farmers, ranchers, cowboys, miners, Membreno Apaches, and Utes from miles around – were gathered along the race course. For the first time in the four years there had been a San Juan and a Fourth of July race, most of the interest was on someone besides Devlon Gibson and his bay racing mare.

The locals already considered Hayes to be something of a mystery figure. The previous April, the professor, as yet unknown to them, had stepped off the one passenger car of the narrow gauge San Juan Railroad on to the new platform by the depot. The man's immaculately pressed suit and crisp white shirt were a wonder considering that he had just completed a ride of eight hours on the hard wooden benches of the screenless passenger car behind an engine belching smoke and cinders. Without speaking to anyone, the stranger walked directly to the office of Devlon Gibson, President of the San Juan Bank as well as Chairman of the

9

San Juan School Board and informed him that he was applying for the vacant position of teacher at the San Juan School.

Many of the locals hadn't liked the idea of a man teacher but had been swayed by Devlon Gibson's argument that a man wouldn't get married in the first three months and quit as the last three women teachers had done. Also, Hayes' scholarly answers to interview questions in his soft southern drawl had impressed other school board members. Besides, as in most other matters in San Juan, it was Devlon Gibson's vote that counted most.

After being informed that he was hired, Hayes had briefly visited the one-room school and the two-room teacher's house behind it, agreed to start school on the sixth of July, and caught the afternoon train out of town. Until this morning, locals had heard nothing else of Professor Hayes except to receive several heavy boxes labeled 'Books' addressed to A.J. Hayes, San Juan, New Mexico Territory.

Each year, Gibson made it a point to be the last arrival at the starting line for the race. At five minutes until noon, Gibson showed up leading his sleek, clean-limbed bay mare out of Kentucky bloodlines, with a small teenaged Ute boy on her back. Gibson grinned at Doc Ramsey, who still sat in the same chair in front of the Mercantile. 'Looks like the professor had a change of heart, Doc,' Gibson told him.

In response, Doc Ramsey pointed at Hayes emerging from an alley astride the walking horse but leading a spectacular, deep red stallion. Hayes slid from his saddle, dropped his reins, removed his coat, and laid it neatly across the black horse's saddle, placing his hat on top. Thus prepared, he led the red stallion toward the starting line.

The stallion was a little over fifteen hands, had muscles that rippled smoothly with each move and legs that tapered to thin ankles and teacup-sized hoofs. A single white blaze across the side of his face and a scattering of white hairs in his mane were the only change from the deep red coat, which reflected the sun back in fiery tones. Gibson stalked toward the professor, waving his arms and almost shouting, 'What the. . . ? This isn't the same horse. . . .'

'You didn't ask what horse I was racing,' Hayes answered calmly.

Gibson was clearly dumbfounded. 'But I assumed—'

'Assumed?' Hayes asked and arched his eyebrows.

The professor swung easily into the saddle despite his limp when he walked. Immediately, he tightened the reins and held the horse, dancing and twisting, a few feet behind the others. The stallion's sleek muscles quivered eagerly.

'Professor, you know the course?' Doc Ramsey asked as he strolled to the starting line.

Hayes nodded. Doc Ramsey pulled his pistol, checked his watch, and looked toward Gibson, who was still standing in the center of the horses and riders. 'Time to move away, Devlon,' Doc Ramsey told him, his voice soft but businesslike.

Gibson looked from the doc to Hayes. 'But—'

'Fifteen seconds,' Doc Ramsey interrupted.

Gibson stepped forward and raised his hand toward the muscular neck of the red racer. Hayes reined the stallion back. 'No one else handles Red,' he said.

'You better win!' Gibson told the young Ute and pointed his finger as if it were a loaded weapon. Then he stomped angrily toward the side of the street.

Hayes barely managed to hold the excited stallion in check as horses surged forward. At the crack of Doc Ramsey's pistol, Hayes turned the stallion loose and pointed it toward the first opening in the line of the other horses. The stallion shot past all of the horses except

11

Gibson's mare. The two of them exploded down the one street of town, two lengths ahead of the others and gaining steadily. The Ute boy lay almost flat on the bay mare's neck, the wind whipping his hair in a long black stream behind his head. He pounded his heels into the mare's sides and slashed her rump with a leather quirt.

Hayes had neither spurs nor quirt but leaned forward on his horse's neck. The white bark of aspens, the light green of cottonwood foliage, and darker green of firs flashed past in a blur of indistinct shapes. The wind in Hayes' eyes drew tears and immediately whisked them away. The only sounds that Hayes really heard were the drumming of horses' hoofs – at once almost deafening but also pushed to the background – Red gasping in great draughts of air, and a grunting from deep within the red stallion. The professor gloried in the smooth contracting and stretching of the stallion's powerful muscles, their rhythm becoming almost part of his own body. Without conscious thought Hayes shifted his body as the horse raced over the uneven course, horse and man moving as one.

Neither the stallion nor the mare gained on the other until the first turn that carried the riders through a shallow ford of San Juan Creek. The mare splashed quickly through the inside of the turn, moving ahead of Hayes on the outside. Water from the mare's hoofs flew up into the face of Hayes' stallion. It drifted wider into the turn, away from the stinging spray. The mare emerged from the water a length ahead. As Red closed the gap to almost even with the mare, the Ute's quirt barely missed Red's face and spooked him into veering to the outside; he fell behind but quickly surged back. As Hayes urged the stallion past the mare, the Ute slashed his stallion across the nose; flecks of blood flew into Hayes' face. The stallion threw his head up and away and quickly fell two lengths behind the mare. Instead of being cowed, though, Red fought back, as angry as his rider. By the time the horses approached the next turn, Red had opened a length and a half lead against the mare.

The roughly laid out oval course crossed San Juan Creek again between the third and fourth turns, this crossing deeper than the first. Hayes took a look back as Red hit the creek and was surprised to find the mare closing in. As Red started out of the creek, he slipped on a mud-covered rock and floundered awkwardly, almost falling to the ground. Hayes kicked his feet free of the stirrups, caught his left foot on the bank, and lifted himself above Red for a moment as the stallion regained its balance.

Cool air from the creek swept over Hayes almost as if the icy water were bathing him. The mare shot past. Hayes knew he was racing against a special horse, but Red's blazing speed took over down the last straight. The big red thoroughbred stretched out and turned on the fastest burst of speed of his life, gaining as the crowd at the finish line appeared to fly toward the racers. Even before Red had passed the mare, the professor was thinking about the kind of colts that would come from mating Red with the bay mare. In the last fifty yards, the stallion shot into the lead and finished a length ahead of Devlon Gibson's horse.

Hayes let Red slow gradually into a trot to cool his muscles and emotions. By the time he turned his stallion and walked him back to the finish line, the crowd was milling around excitedly. Hayes willed his own pulse to slow as he regained focus. Gibson stormed into the mob, grabbed the Ute boy from the mare and threw him roughly down into the street. 'Get away! Stay away!' Gibson screamed at the youth.

The boy bounced back to his feet and crouched, his weight on the balls of his feet, glaring at Devlon Gibson. His hand was poised near a bulge underneath the seam of his loose-fitting cotton shirt. Hayes slid to the ground beside the Ute. 'Hey!' he exclaimed loudly enough to break into the youth's attention. 'Walk that mare out for me. Whatever he paid you, I'll pay.'

The boy glared at Gibson for another moment, straightened, and walked the mare away. The boy's shirt flared open far enough for Hayes to see the handle of an old muzzle-loading pistol thrust into his belt.

Gibson suddenly seemed to become aware that everyone was staring at him. For another moment, he struggled visibly to gain control of his emotions, then finally extended his hand toward Hayes and spoke in a strained voice. 'Great race and a great horse, Professor.'

Hayes quickly grasped Gibson's hand. Gibson tried to crunch Hayes hand, but turned redder when he realized that Hayes had protected himself by the grip he had taken. 'I'll pay you a thousand dollars for the pair – my Eva and your red stallion,' Gibson offered through a tight smile.

People gasped; no one had ever heard of such a price for horses in New Mexico.

'Neither is for sale,' Hayes answered levelly.

'Two thousand,' Gibson offered and tried again to crush Hayes' hand.

The murmur from the crowd grew. 'No sale at any price,' Hayes responded and looked pointedly at their clasped hands. Eyes of those in the crowd followed Hayes' eyes. Gibson reluctantly released Hayes' hand.

'Doc Ramsey is holding the money,' Gibson said, his voice sounding like he had difficulty forcing the words out. He scanned the crowd nervously with his eyes, and stalked stiffly away. Spectators lingered until the sound of a cook clanging a metal bar on a triangle drew them away.

The Ute boy led the mare up beside Hayes, took Red's reins without being told to do so, and walked both down the street to cool them gradually. Hayes watched in surprise. No one else had ever been able to handle Red, but now the stallion followed the Ute boy as meekly as a pet.

'One hundred dollars' prize and Devlon's three hundred,' Ramsey said as he handed money to the professor.

Hayes handed the five double eagles back to Ramsey and dropped the remainder into his pocket. 'I'll take the same bag of gold I gave Mr Gibson.'

'Does it matter?' Doc Ramsey asked as the two of them walked toward the professor's black walking horse.

Hayes took time to button his coat neatly before he looked Doc Ramsey directly in the eye and replied, 'It matters.'

Doc Ramsey nodded his acceptance and dropped the five gold pieces in his pocket. 'The mare's name is Eva,' he told Hayes. 'Named after Devlon's late mother.'

Hayes' and Ramsey's boot heels echoed hollowly on the sidewalks now that the crowd had moved to the shady trees by the depot where the cooks were beginning to serve food. Through the glass window in the door of the bank, Hayes saw Devlon Gibson and another large man, very dark with a pitted face, bending intently over a large desk. The sound of the door opening appeared to startle both. Gibson attempted to appear casual as he sat some papers over the item he and the other man had been examining on his desk. Hayes hadn't met the other man but recognized him to be Pitt Hudson, the operator of the Shady Lady, a bordello on the outskirts of San Juan. Both turned their bodies to shield the objects on the table.

'Professor Hayes would prefer to keep the gold he gave you for his wager,' Doc Ramsey announced as he laid the five gold eagles on the table.

Gibson's face flushed. 'I—' The big banker caught

himself. 'Wait outside.'

Hayes looked back over his shoulder as he went out the door and saw Pitt Hudson using his knife blade to scrape the flakes and kernels of gold back into Hayes' leather bag. Hayes could see from the expression on Doc Ramsey's face that he had also noticed. After a moment, the door opened and Gibson handed Hayes his bag. The teacher opened the bag to look inside and nodded. 'Thankyou,' he said formally. Gibson greeted the thanks with stony-faced silence.

'Devlon's a better friend than enemy,' Doc Ramsey said as they walked away.

'I have no desire to make an enemy,' Hayes answered in a matter of fact tone.

'He's a mighty prideful man,' Doc said, 'but people here like him.'

The terrible loneliness that Hayes had so often felt washed strongly over him. He walked for another moment, trying unsuccessfully to get rid of the lonely ache before stepping toward the serving line at the barbecue. The professor turned toward Doc Ramsey. 'I want to live here in peace, Doctor Ramsey.' He paused and turned his eyes directly to those of the doctor. 'I didn't intend to push Gibson so hard.'

CHAPTER THREE

The crowd gathered by the depot awaited the third major event of the Fourth of July even more eagerly than the race and the big feast. A banner draped from one end of the depot to the other, proclaimed, 'Welcome Ladies!'

Like most western towns of the 1860s, San Juan was predominately male, with a large percentage of the small female population made up of Pitt Hudson's 'soiled doves' of the Shady Lady, San Juan's only nearby bordello. The very small number of 'decent women' was a common topic of conversation among the handful of wives in San Juan. San Juan's biggest need, they agreed, was the civilizing influence of a greater number of decent women. Devlon Gibson, himself a bachelor, had responded to this idea by putting up the money to advertise in eastern and mid-western newspapers and pay expenses for single women and widows with matrimony in mind to relocate to San Juan.

The bachelors in the crowd were dressed in their best and had dipped into the kegs of free beer and whiskey much more lightly than usual. The small knot of married women who gathered on one corner of the depot platform took this improved appearance and demeanor as confirmation of the civilizing influence of the additional women soon to arrive. Eager suitors stood near the center of the platform, alternately boisterous and shy. Pitt Hudson lounged against the corner of the depot opposite the wives. Hudson was almost as large as Devlon Gibson; his swarthy, pock-marked skin and Indian-dark hair gave him a hard appearance. Several of Hudson's gaily dressed 'doves' remained further back from the platform, leaning against a large surrey. Devlon Gibson, apparently recovered of his good humor after the horse race, bustled up with the Bible-toting minister of San Juan's one church ready at hand for instant weddings.

A cheer went up from all the groups as the dim sound of a whistle sounded at the same time that smoke first appeared in Toltec Pass through which the narrow gauge San Juan-Toltec Railroad connected San Juan to the outside world. Excitement grew as the shiny engine, trimmed in red and gold, popped into view. Steel rubbing on steel squealed as the brakes locked to slow the train. The one freshly painted red passenger car, located just behind the coal car, traveled on past the depot, leaving a momentary empty feeling in the gathered crowd. Fifty yards past the depot, the train finally managed to skid to a stop. For a moment, the train sat maddeningly still. After what seemed a very long time to the spectators, ever so slowly, the wheels began to inch backwards and pick up a bit of speed as the passenger car approached, backing toward the platform. The brakes locked again; the passenger car jerked to a sudden, clamorous stop. Great plumes of steam obscured the train as the engineer vented the lines. A moment seemed to linger forever before events began to unfold.

Finally, the agent from the depot, for once dressed in a black suit and flat-crowned cap, bustled out, dropped a step from the deck at the back of the passenger car and reached inside the door for another step to sit on the platform. After what seemed to the townspeople to be an eternal wait, the agent stood, straightened his cap, and announced grandly, 'San Juan, New Mexico Territory!'

Still, nothing seemed to be happening until the billows of steam began to thin enough that the San Juan townspeople could see through the windows to make out figures filing through the passenger car toward the back door. After another long minute or so, women began to emerge on to the narrow platform at the back of the passenger car, most coming shyly, their eyes averted from the waiting crowd.

Devlon Gibson gave each an assisting hand down to the platform and spoke quiet words of welcome. Groups around the edge of the platform chattered and laughed while the formerly eager bachelors and the eligible women stood facing each other in awkward silence. The twentieth and last woman to step down on to the depot platform was a tall strawberry blonde with very light skin and a few noticeable freckles.

Devlon Gibson, towering inches taller than everyone except Pitt Hudson, walked to the middle of the platform. The groups fell silent. 'We welcome all of you ladies to San Juan,' Gibson announced. 'We are proud of our town but feel it needs more of a lady's touch and the sound of children.' Gibson pointed to the parson. 'Reverend Gooden will be glad to direct each of you to accommodations for tonight if you don't make other arrangements by then.' Watchers laughed. 'He is also prepared to perform matrimony for those so inclined,' Gibson concluded and stepped away.

The observers around the edge of the platform applauded. For a moment, no one moved but finally several men broke away from the bachelors' group, self-consciously approached the women, and began low conversations. The wives present grumbled audibly when Pitt Hudson strode on to the platform and approached one saucy-looking, red-haired woman. The woman listened to Hudson for a moment and then happily accompanied him to join the other women from the Shady Lady. A.J. Hayes stood alone, acutely aware of his loneliness amidst this crowd, a sense which became even sharper as pairs of newly met men and women began to leave together.

The crowd stirred again as Pitt Hudson re-entered the mixing of bachelors and new women, now down to only a few, and approached the tall young woman who had been the last to emerge from the train. She was at least five feet eight inches, with shoulder-length hair and large green eyes. Her clothes were of coarse, inexpensive cloth but were well made and neat. The loose fit of those clothes didn't hide the shapeliness of the young woman, who appeared to be probably no more than eighteen or nineteen years old. Pitt Hudson towered over the other potential suitors and glared malevolently until each finally turned away. Hudson spoke to the young woman, much as he had to the saucy redhead, but this woman stepped backwards, her mouth forming an angry, 'No!' Hudson stepped closer and fastened his big hand on her elbow. The woman jerked away and turned from him. The big man smiled confidently at her. Another man, a miner by his laced boots, then approached her.

Hayes thought he saw purposeful eye contact between Hudson and Devlon Gibson and was almost certain that Gibson had nodded slightly toward Hudson. But Hayes chided himself that perhaps he was too quick to find fault with Gibson. Hudson glared down at the miner, a small man with graying hair, and spoke to him under his breath. The miner appeared to try to resist the big man but gave in to Hudson's threat and moved away.

The depot platform began to empty. Most of the women had left with one or another of the men. A few others gathered around the minister. The minister, a tall, gaunt man with a clerical collar under his prominent Adam's apple, separated himself and approached the remaining woman. Pitt Hudson cut in and spoke quietly but angrily to the minister. The minister then spoke but briefly with the young woman without making eye contact before returning to his group. Hayes felt as if he were watching a cut flower wilt in hot sunlight as he observed the minister.

Hudson spoke once again to the woman and received no answer other than silence and a stony stare straight ahead. He nevertheless hung around her, standing with his arms crossed, a confident grin on his face.

'Pitt Hudson is a dangerous man.' Hayes had been so engrossed in watching the woman and Hudson that he had neither heard Doc Ramsey approach nor smelled the glass of whiskey in his hand. For just a moment, it flashed into Hayes' mind that he had yet to see the level of whiskey in

Doc Ramsey's glass vary, but his attention quickly returned to the events on the depot platform.

Professor Hayes hadn't realized what he was going to do until he felt himself moving toward Pitt Hudson and the woman. His first thought was that the woman was even taller than he had thought, at least three or more inches taller than he. He was aware that she was looking at him as if waiting to see what he was going to do, but he had no more idea than she. As the professor began to speak, one part of him seemed to be an interested bystander listening to discover what the other part was going to do. Hayes removed his hat and offered her his hand. 'A.J. Hayes, ma'am. Do you have plans?'

She didn't look surprised at the question nor flustered by the situation. She placed her hand lightly in his and answered as levelly and as calmly as she might have commented on the weather, 'I came to be married.'

Hayes didn't take his eyes off of her, but couldn't miss seeing Pitt Hudson drop his hands angrily to his side and move closer. Hayes felt the flush of anger that a bully always evoked in him. He must remember, Hayes reminded himself, not to create a situation that would endanger the young woman. Hayes simply ignored Hudson.

Neither the woman's hand nor her voice registered the slightest quiver. The woman's poise under stress impressed him. Again, Hayes listened to himself speak, almost as if he were one of the spectators. 'I am a teacher, although I have other plans for the future. It is the school's house in which I live. It is simple but well built.' Hayes paused for a moment. 'I'm perhaps old enough to be your father, but I'm a very lonely man. I would treat you with the respect and dignity a wife deserves. What I am trying to say Miss. . . .'

'McNew. Rachel McNew,' the young woman filled in.

Hudson interrupted. 'Little man, you're asking for more trouble than you could handle even if you weren't a cripple.'

Hayes didn't respond to Hudson except to take a moment to look directly into the eyes of the big man before turning his attention back to Rachel McNew. Hudson sneered toward the woman. 'Did you notice that the little school marm is crippled?'

Rachel looked back at Hudson for the first time since refusing his earlier offer. 'I noticed that Mr Hayes is a gentleman. And I'm asking,' her eyes swung back to Hayes, 'as my wedding present, that he ignore you.'

Hayes placed his hat back on to his head and offered his left arm to Rachel. With his right hand, he touched his hat brim to Hudson. 'Until another day, Mr Hudson.' Hayes picked up the one carpetbag that was Rachel McNew's only luggage, noticing from the weight that it was almost empty. The professor could hardly believe that the situation was real as he escorted Rachel McNew away from the depot platform. *This must be part of a dream*, he told himself. *I'll soon be waking up.* He pressed his left arm against his side and found Rachel McNew's hand there to be solid and real enough.

The professor observed the young woman out of the corner of his eye as they left the platform. Rachel McNew held herself proudly erect rather than slumping as many tall women would do in order to avoid appearing to be taller than the man by her side. It was so strange to think that he was about to marry this woman he didn't know, but he felt pride in her erect carriage and the steel she had shown in defying Pitt Hudson. *After all, how well do many men know a woman who they have courted in stiffly formal settings?* Hayes mused. *I have seen Rachel McNew show backbone and grace in an extremely tense situation.* A.J. Hayes decided that he liked the decision he had so quickly made.

The town ladies who remained near the platform turned their backs disapprovingly as Hayes and Rachel strode off the platform. Two fluffy white clouds floated in the deep blue of the high desert skies.

Already, the afternoon breeze was becoming cooler. A fire would feel good by evening at this elevation. Trace chains rattled as the mules hitched to a wagon parked in front of the depot grew impatient.

'Would you prefer some time to get to know me before the wedding?' Hayes asked as they walked.

Rachel stopped dead still in the middle of the street and stood erect, her eyes straight ahead. 'Do you regret asking me to marry you?' she asked.

'No,' Hayes responded calmly. 'I just don't want to rush you.'

'How long will it take us to walk to the church?' she asked, staring ahead.

It was Hayes turn to wonder. 'Maybe three minutes,' he responded.

'If I don't tell you differently by then, I'm ready,' Rachel told him and stepped forward toward the church. Hayes stepped quickly so as not to be left behind. He had to stretch his normal stride to stay abreast of Rachel and suppressed an urge to laugh aloud at their exchange.

A knot of people, several of the men dressed in white shirts and ties for the big Fourth of July celebration, stood around the church, the only whitewashed building in San Juan. The minister, who had faded under Pitt Hudson's glare at the depot, watched Rachel McNew and A.J. Hayes approach. The minister was almost six feet tall and very bony in appearance. His dark blonde hair streamed toward the shoulders of his gray suit. Gray, Hayes decided, was an appropriate color for this man. Hayes touched the brim of his hat to the ladies and spoke directly to the point. 'Reverend. . . .'

The minister finally realized that Professor Hayes was asking his name. 'Gooden, Jonathan Gooden,' the minister responded. 'Parishioners call me Brother Johnnie.'

'Reverend Gooden,' Professor Hayes continued, 'this is Rachel McNew. I am A.J. Hayes. We wish to be married.'

The preacher glanced nervously at the people who stood watching and back to the couple. 'When?' he finally responded.

'Now,' Hayes answered evenly.

The preacher squirmed uncomfortably, his eyes turning everywhere except toward the couple. The professor watched for what seemed a long time before he broke the silence. 'It was my understanding that you were marrying couples.'

Brother Johnnie continued to squirm. 'Yes, but. . . .' He left the sentence hanging.

Hayes stared levelly at the preacher, who kept his eyes uneasily averted. 'But what?' he asked, his soft drawl not masking the sternness of his mood.

Brother Johnnie continued to stumble. 'But, well . . . the others weren't the teacher,' he finally concluded.

'I wasn't told that the teacher had to be unmarried,' Hayes replied. He wasn't going to give Brother Johnnie any respite; if he hadn't found him so contemptible, he might have felt sorry for him. Instead, he let his hard glare press the preacher.

Brother Johnnie finally replied, 'It just isn't seemly marrying this way, you being the teacher and all.'

'It would have been more seemly to allow Miss McNew to be left to the mercy of Pitt Hudson, I suppose?' he asked, his voice still level but now cutting.

Brother Johnnie's face looked like he had been kicked

in the groin. Hayes knew Brother Johnnie would never forgive him for mentioning in front of his parishioners the weakness he had shown before Pitt Hudson. 'As you wish,' Brother Johnnie finally answered, resigned to what he had to do.

A small woman, her white hair almost covered by a light blue bonnet edged with homemade white lace, stepped forward from the knot of bystanders. Like Rachel, her clothing was well made but of inexpensive fabric. She extended a brown, work-hardened hand toward Rachel McNew. 'I'm Hattie Gillis. Welcome to San Juan,' she offered. A broad smile split her face, deeply tanned despite the bonnet. Hayes was struck by the grace with which the lady moved. Rachel hesitated only a moment before she turned loose of the professor's arm and took Hattie's hand. 'Rachel McNew,' she said.

A man of medium height and heavy build, his coal-black hair graying around the ears, stepped forward. 'My husband, Angus,' Hattie added.

'We'd be happy to stand up as witnesses for you, if you have no one else,' Angus Gillis added, a touch of a Scottish brogue in his voice.

Professor Hayes accepted the thick, callused hand. 'Miss McNew and I would be honored,' he replied.

Other bystanders turned away and left, disapproval readily seen in their faces. 'I'll swannie, Hattie,' one said loudly enough for Hayes to overhear. 'Sometimes you beat all.'

The four members of the wedding party followed Brother Johnnie into the church, Hayes and Angus Gillis trailing the women. 'After all,' Angus added quietly, 'I suspect we're going to be neighbors in the future.'

Hayes looked in quick surprise at Gillis, but the Scotsman walked on with a smug smile and a twinkle in his eye. Before Hayes could ponder Gillis's statement, he found himself positioned to Rachel's right facing Brother Johnnie. Angus Gillis stood beside the professor, Hattie beside Rachel.

Rachel's hand tightened excitedly on Hayes' arm. 'An organ!'

Hayes followed her gleaming eyes. A polished oak pump organ sat pushed against the wall in the corner as if out of use. 'No one in our congregation plays,' Hattie said.

'I love. . . .' Rachel's voice trailed away as Brother Johnnie stepped into the pulpit facing the wedding party. He took his black Bible from a low wooden railing that separated the pulpit from the church. Hayes noticed how long and thin the minister's fingers were, stroking the Bible as if attempting to draw strength. Brother Johnnie drew to his full height as if being back in his accustomed setting had stiffened his backbone.

Ten benches made from rough-sewn lumber graced the small church. The wonder of the church, for New Mexico, was two sets of glass windows, which graced each side wall. Hayes noticed how tightly fitted the rough-sawn lumber was. Skilled hands had done the inside finish work on the church, Hayes noticed with approval.

'Professor Hayes, Miss McNew,' Brother Johnnie began, now in his pulpit voice, 'understand that I consider marriage to be a fine idea, one of God's institutions. It just seems undignified, under these circumstances, for the teacher.' The minister looked down on the couple from his slightly elevated pulpit. 'How old are you, Miss McNew?' he asked, disapproval in his voice.

Rachel, Hayes realized, seemed completely at ease. 'Seventeen,' she answered.

Hayes was surprised but didn't allow his expression or eyes to waver. Brother Johnnie looked back to Hayes, his demeanor no longer nervous. 'That is no older than some of your students, Professor.'

'Two years older than I was,' Hattie Gillis broke in as she placed her hand reassuringly on Rachel's arm. The professor didn't respond to the preacher.

Brother Johnnie directed his gaze at Rachel. 'Are your parents aware of what you are doing?'

'My parents are dead,' Rachel answered calmly.

'Other members of your family?' Brother Johnnie continued.

'I have . . . I had no one.' She leaned slightly against the professor's shoulder as she answered.

Brother Johnnie nodded. 'You've never been married?'

'No,' she responded evenly.

'Then let us continue,' the minister began with reservation in his voice. 'Dearly beloved. . . .'

CHAPTER FOUR

The inside of Gibson's Mercantile smelled of leather, new cloth, spices, salted meat, and tobacco. Every shelf was packed full, and many items hung suspended from rafters. The professor had seen many larger towns that didn't have a store so well stocked.

A short, rounded man with a bald pate stepped from behind a counter, wiping his hands on his long white apron. The green elastic band around his sleeve, Hayes noted, was stretched tight. The storekeeper had a more muscular arm than one expected on a storekeeper who otherwise looked soft and rounded.

'Professor Hayes, Mrs Hayes, I'm Robert Parker.' The man nodded but didn't offer a handshake. 'Welcome to San Juan.' His dour face didn't match his words.

Hayes nodded. Rachel walked to the rack with bolts of cloth and stared as if mesmerized by the rainbow of colors and patterns. Her hand lingered lovingly on a bolt of rich indigo velvet until she noticed her husband watching. She wandered down the shelves taking in the abundance of goods admiringly, touching many, until she noticed the professor at her elbow.

'I'll need your help selecting,' Hayes told her, emotion rising close to the surface. 'I've never helped set up a real home before.'

Rachel seemed pleased, but as she looked at pots and pans and dishes, she hesitated about decisions. Finally, Hayes showed a handful of gold coins. 'It has been a very profitable day. Buy what you would really like.'

She began picking items, quickly and efficiently putting together an order, every item something necessary, picking out good quality but not necessarily the most expensive items. Rachel's eyes quickly darted once more toward the cloth rack and quickly away. The professor walked to the cloth rack and looked back to his wife. 'This, I think,' he said as he laid his hand on the indigo velvet, 'would be lovely with your hair and eyes.'

He had no idea what the cloth cost, but the expression on Rachel's face would make the money well spent. Finally, a substantial pile of supplies, including several selections of cloth, lay stacked on the counter. Hayes paid in gold coin.

'We also buy raw gold.' Devlon Gibson's voice surprised them both. Hayes noted how quietly the big man had approached.

'Nice to know,' Hayes responded blandly. Rachel looked from one to the other. 'You deliver, I presume?' Hayes asked.

Gibson nodded and followed the two outside. In the street outside, the Ute boy held the reins to Napoleon, Red, and the racing mare won from Gibson. Hayes glanced up at Gibson, went to the bay mare, stripped off the lightweight racing saddle, and dropped it on the sidewalk in front of Devlon Gibson without saying a word to him.

'Are these yours?' Rachel asked as she stared at the horses, barely controlled excitement in her eyes.

Hayes nodded. Rachel stepped off the sidewalk and slowly circled the horses. Hayes watched her eyes as they knowingly appraised the animals. She ran her hands down the leg of the bay mare, fingering the pastern and the fetlocks. Engrossed, she touched her shoulder lightly against the front quarter of the mare and tapped her on the leg, took the raised foot and ran her fingers around on the inside of the hoof, brushing sand from the frog of the foot. She lowered the mare's foot and patted her gently on her shoulder. Her eyes glowed with excitement as she straightened and looked toward the professor.

'Kentucky?' she asked as she pointed at the two thoroughbreds.

Hayes nodded again.

'My goodness!' Rachel said breathlessly. 'They're magnificent!'

Rachel held her hand out for the mare and Red to smell and ran her hand down the mare's neck and scratched the top of her neck under the mane. Next she reached toward Red.

'Be care—' Hayes stopped as Red stretched his neck to be stroked by the lady. Twice in one day, Red had allowed someone else to touch him, in fact had behaved like a pet. Perhaps he was dreaming all of this, he decided.

'Your lady has an eye and a touch for the horses, Professor,' Devlon Gibson remarked, as he bit the end off of a slim cigar.

Hayes felt his face redden at the way Devlon Gibson's eyes ran up and down Rachel's shapely body.

'The mare's name,' Hayes told Rachel, 'is Eva. She is your wedding present.'

'You must have expected more when you boarded the train for New Mexico,' Hayes said. Rachel had related her story of the loss of her family, a stepfather who had begun to make improper advances after her mother's death, and how she had taken the 'marriage train' on a whim to get away.

She laid her hand on top of the professor's and leaned forward. 'I hoped for a man who would treat me kindly and who I could respect,' she told him warmly. 'I'm happier tonight than in years.'

They touched for the first time since they had entered the house. Hayes felt new warmth reaching deep within him. He wanted to believe that Rachel would continue to feel the same but looked at her and saw a young girl, no older than several who he would greet in class on Monday. He felt the doubt creeping back in. *She is just so young. So very young!*

Hayes rose. 'It's late. . . .' He felt as awkward as a boy with his first girlfriend. He looked away and began picking up the coffee cups on the table. 'You sleep in there,' he nodded his head toward the bedroom door without really looking. 'I'll pitch a pallet out here.'

Rachel looked up, surprise obvious in her face. 'Are you sorry you married me?'

Hayes didn't meet her eyes. 'No. I'm. . . . We know so. . . . It's just that you're so. . . .' The normally assured professor struggled with his words.

'I'm so young?' Rachel finished.

He finally looked into her eyes. 'Yes.'

Rachel walked around the table to her husband and took his hand once again and raised it to her lips. 'I'm a married woman and happy to be so,' she told him softly. By his hand, she led him toward their bedroom, slowing to blow out the one lantern. Moonlight streamed through the windows. Wind fluttered the curtains away from the wall. 'We're either going to be a married couple or not,' Rachel told him.

She dropped his hand and began to unbutton her dress. 'I'm qualified to be a blushing bride,' she told him as her dress dropped to the floor. 'I'm just not the blushing type.'

The filtered moonlight from the open window high-lighted full breasts and womanly curves, her face deep in shadow. The professor stood dry-mouthed, staring but not moving. Rachel took his hand and lifted it to her lips for a soft kiss. Hayes' hand lingered a moment and slid down her neck and her side to the curves of her hips. Rachel leaned forward for their first kiss. Hayes pulled Rachel against himself, his heart racing. After the kiss, Rachel stepped away and lay, outlined in the dim light across the bed, her hand gently leading A.J. Hayes to her side.

'I'm new at all this, Professor Hayes,' she told him in a soft, teasing voice, 'but I think you need to take off your boots.'

CHAPTER FIVE

Squeals of fear split the peaceful hollow surrounded by the white trunks and spring green leaves of July aspens in the New Mexico high country. 'Stop! Those hurt. Mr Hayes!'

The big 16-year-old, black-haired, rough-skinned boy

laughed tauntingly at the younger boy. 'Mr Hayes. Mr Hayes. Call on a half-pint cripple.'

The other oversized boy, his worn butternut pants held up by one leather strap over a rough red linsey-woolsey shirt, threw another big clod of dirt from beside the new well. Wind ruffled his long bright red hair. 'Yeah, you scare Ory and me calling on Mr Hayes.'

Rusty Tucker pulled his one leather strap back into place and threw another dirt clod. Two younger boys and a girl tried to hide behind the trunk of the huge cottonwood tree in the schoolyard. The smallest 6-year-old boy grabbed his cheek and fell to the ground as red dirt shattered around his face. Ory grabbed his side laughing and reached for a new clod.

'Ory and Rusty, stop that now!'

Ory and Rusty stopped for a moment, mainly because they were surprised that the new teacher had learned their names on his first day of school. They quickly recovered, though, and reached for two more fist-sized clods.

'Why yes sir, Mr New Teacher,' Rusty laughed sarcastically.

'Put them down!' Hayes said in a level but authoritative voice.

Rusty looked at the teacher, at least five inches shorter than his six feet and forty pounds lighter than his one hundred ninety pounds. In addition to being smaller, the boys had noticed that he dragged his left foot when he walked, creating a slight limp. Rusty and Ory looked at each other and laughed out loud as they flung the clods toward the small children. Two explosions rocked the clearing almost at the same moment. Dirt flying from the shattered clods stung the older boys' faces. Both fell to the ground. In the door of the school, Professor Hayes lowered two Navy Colt revolvers, smoke drifting around his waist. 'That will be quite enough of your rowdiness. Inside for mathematics.'

Children stared. Ory picked himself up from the ground and wiped the red dirt from his eyes. Awe was in his voice as well as his face. 'Wow! One with each hand. That's shooting!'

Rusty Tucker lowered his hand, looking at the small amount of blood from where a shattered pebble had scratched his neck. 'You shot me! I'm going for my pa! You've had it, Cripple!' Rusty's bare feet kicked up puffs of red dust as he ran into the aspen.

'Inside for mathematics,' the professor repeated.

None of the boys missed the way that their new teacher tucked the two pistols out of sight under his long black frock coat. They memorized details so they could tell the story of what had happened better than anyone else. The man's face was surprisingly tanned for a teacher, more noticeable in contrast against the crisp white shirt and starched collar. His frame wasn't heavy but the boys' more careful second looks revealed that he wasn't nearly as slight as they first thought. The black tie was tied with a modest sized bow and long tails. His black boots shone from careful shining.

By the time the children were settled on their split log benches, Professor Hayes had written on the big black slate board in precise, even letters: Euclid. 'Ladies and gentlemen,' Andrew Jackson Hayes began in his soft southern tones, 'I don't intend to ask you twice to behave. Please don't forget,' he paused and looked the class over, managing to make eye contact with each of the eleven students remaining, 'we will begin to study geometry today. Geometry is one of the most practical subjects, as you will learn.'

The small teacher paused as Ory Pickett raised his hand, an anxious look on his face. 'Yes, Ory?'

Ory quickly stood. 'Mr Hayes, you might better ride out of here. Curt Tucker's mine isn't more than five miles.'

Professor Hayes waited a moment as if he expected more information. 'Yes, Ory, I know where the CT is located.'

'But Mr Hayes,' Ory blurted, 'Rusty's pa is the meanest man in San Juan. He'll be some het up about your scraping Rusty's face.'

'Heated. Heated is the past tense of heat, not het. And I'm sure that Mr Tucker is a reasonable man.' He turned toward the board and began the geometry lesson.

As soon as school was dismissed, every child raced to try to be the first to tell about Professor Hayes shooting two dirt clods out of the air and about Rusty's bloodied face. The professor quickly tidied up the classroom, then took an oaken bucket to the well and drew water to take to the two-room house in which he lived behind the one-room school.

The professor noted what seemed an unusual number of persons standing idly on the short street of San Juan as he rode Napoleon directly to the hitching rack in front of the Gilded Lily, San Juan's one saloon. He straightened his hat and smiled slightly at the consternation he saw in several of the town's ladies as he strode toward the open door of the saloon. He hadn't failed to notice Devlon Gibson and Pitt Hudson watching from the window of the bank across the street.

A.J. Hayes looked neither left nor right as he strode directly to the bar of the Gilded Lily. It took a moment for his eyes to adjust from the bright afternoon sun to the unlighted dimness of the saloon. A bartender started toward the teacher but turned back as a woman walked up to Hayes. 'Professor, you do seem determined to agitate the good townspeople. Gambling, marrying strange little girls, now coming into this den of iniquity.' She shook her head in mock despair.

Hayes immediately liked the woman. She was small, several inches shorter than he. Chestnut brown hair fell in elaborately curled ringlets to her bare shoulders. Neither coloring nor hairstyle attempted to conceal the graying on the left side of her head. The healthy freshly scrubbed look of her skin and clear brown eyes matched neither the setting nor her low cut red satin dress. 'I suppose none of the respectable men of San Juan come to your place?' Hayes queried with a relaxed smile.

'Almost all,' she responded.

'But I shouldn't?'

'Two persons that people don't want to find next to them at the bar,' she said, 'are their preacher and their child's teacher.' The woman laughed easily and softly as she turned up a glass in front of the professor.

'Brandy?' Hayes asked.

'Would you expect less in an elegant establishment catering to successful entrepreneurs and scholars?' she countered as she pulled out a bottle from under the bar and poured a small glassful.

Hayes sniffed approvingly. 'Join me?'

'Never touch liquor or other women's husbands,' she responded.

Much of the woman's attraction, A.J. considered, was that she kept intense eye contact with him, which he found unusual in a woman. It would be something that she did instinctively rather than to signal attraction to a man, he decided. Hayes sipped the brandy as he watched the mirror out of the corner of his eye, noting how many men had drifted into the saloon since he had arrived. He saw two men standing in the door look excitedly down the street and elbow each other. 'I think I have business,' Hayes told the woman as he began to lay a coin on the bar.

Her hand stopped him and lingered for just a moment, warm on his. 'This one's on Gaye McWilliams. Don't be in here too often, Professor. I think I like you.'

Hayes touched the brim of his hat and walked outside, still feeling her warmth on his hand. Rusty Tucker and an even larger image of Rusty strode purposefully down the street toward the Gilded Lily. The elder Tucker was no taller than Rusty, but a heavier, more massive, older and tougher-looking version of his son. Rusty strutted behind his father, gloating at other students who stood on the sidewalk watching. The angry man planted himself, feet wide apart, hands on his hips in front of Professor Hayes. 'You the little per-fessor that bloodied my boy?'

'I'm A.J. Hayes.'

The miner's face turned deeper red. 'No one messes with my boy,' Curt Tucker practically roared.

Hayes' voice remained a soft southern drawl. 'I have no desire to do anything to Rusty,' Hayes responded, 'if he will behave.'

'You shot him!'

'I shot a clod of dirt he was throwing at small children,' Hayes replied calmly.

The big red-haired man raged. 'You have no business shooting at my boy!'

'If I had shot at Rusty, I would have hit him,' Hayes responded positively.

'I'm going to whip you, and then stomp you down into this dust,' the big man told Hayes and stepped forward.

Hayes held his palm up toward Tucker. 'One moment, please, Mr Tucker.' Tucker stopped in surprise. He wasn't accustomed to people remaining calm when he threatened them. Hayes removed his coat, carefully folded it and laid it across a hitching rail. He then took his hat off and sat it on top of his coat.

'Curt Tucker! Why don't you behave?'

Hayes was surprised that the big voice came from such a small woman. 'Please don't interfere, Miss McWilliams,' Hayes asked politely.

Hayes stepped in front of Tucker, appearing tiny in contrast to the massive miner. 'I'm ready now, Mr Tucker,' Hayes politely told him.

Tucker seemed momentarily put off by Hayes' actions. 'He shot at me,' Rusty reminded his father. The big man growled deep within his chest like an angry bull and lunged toward the professor. Hayes stepped deftly aside and clubbed the back of the miner's neck with doubled fists as he went past. Curt Tucker found himself on his knees shaking his head.

'All of this really isn't necessary, Mr Tucker,' Hayes told him patiently, 'if you will make your son behave himself.' The big man, still on his knees, turned himself toward Hayes, yelled again, lunged off the ground and charged with his head down. This time, Hayes didn't sidestep. Instead he drove his right knee upward and met Curt Tucker's nose, splattering blood outward in a circle. The collision also dropped Hayes to the ground. He rolled over awkwardly and struggled up. Tucker saw this and launched his full two hundred fifteen pounds airborne toward the professor, eager to pin the small man while he was off balance.

Hayes caught his foot in the miner's chest and rolled backwards, grabbing both fists full of Tucker's red hair. Hayes rolled back and thrust with his good right leg. Tucker's own weight carried him over as Hayes thrust hard with his right leg and threw the big miner far past him in the air. Tucker landed flat on his back and whoofed like a bear hit with a rifle slug. Hayes took his time getting to his feet. Tucker desperately struggled to get air back into his lungs as he lingered on his knees.

'Pa, he shot at me,' Rusty's voice reminded plaintively. The boy's voice spurred Curt Tucker back to his feet. This time, the big man slowly closed toward the professor, careful not to have his power sapped by more tricks. Hayes stepped forward and landed a quick jab to Tucker's right cheek. Tucker's head snapped back with the impact of the blow. Hayes backed out of range. Tucker planted his feet widely apart, arms spread as if to insure that the little man didn't get around him. His eyes darkened and he eased forward carefully, gathering his weight on the balls of his feet. Hayes' right foot flicked out quickly, driving his boot heel through Curt Tucker's knee cap. Tucker collapsed like he had been shot and rolled on to his back grimacing with pain.

'Come on, Pa!' Rusty yelled at his father.

Curt Tucker rolled back to one knee. 'You shut up, Rusty! Just shut up!' The big man climbed back on to his feet and swiped his hand across his bloody face, his right knee wobbly. Something rippling in the wind attracted Tucker's attention toward his feet. He reached down and pulled something from under his boot and held it up to look. His eyes grew big in amazement; he burst out into a huge roar of laughter as he held his hand out for everyone to see a thick tuft of his own red hair snatched out when Hayes had flipped him.

'I'll be danged, Professor,' Tucker exclaimed as he hobbled forward and held out his hand. 'I believe you. If you had shot at Rusty, you would have hit him.'

Hayes took the big hand and shook warmly. Tucker whirled and grabbed Rusty before he could get away. 'Boy, you better do what this man says,' Tucker's voice rumbled. 'And I do mean *man!*'

Across the street in front of the San Juan Bank, Mrs Ethlyn Carter, one of the most prominent ladies of the town, shook her finger at Devlon Gibson. 'What have you brought here to teach our young folks, Devlon? He's gambled, married a young girl in most questionable circumstances, hung out in the saloon, and now brawled publicly in the street. What did you get for us?'

Devlon Gibson flicked his cigar stub into the street. 'More than I knew, Mrs Carter. More than I knew.'

CHAPTER SIX

'Yah. Yah,' Sheriff Swede Kittelson told the professor. 'I see nothing else you could have done other than defend yourself. Some of the wives will talk, but I see nothing that can be done about it. It is part of the town wives' job to talk, kind of like your job to teach and mine to keep order.'

The professor had gone to the sheriff's office after sharing a couple of drinks with Curt Tucker and others after his fight. He had found the sheriff at his house on the outskirts of town. While the professor had briefly met and exchanged pleasantries with the sheriff, this was his first time for real business. He had found the sheriff puttering with one of the inventions with which he spent much of his time, today a small windmill, with blades of approximately four feet on a tower approximately twelve feet high. As the blades whirred in the wind, a pushrod manipulated a device of the sheriff's own developing which worked a pump that brought water in a small stream into a trough in his mule pen. The professor was struck with how important such a device could be in the southwest where distance to natural surface water was so scattered as to limit the possibility of grazing the nutrient-rich grasses.

The sheriff stood three or four inches taller than the professor; he was of medium build and had the light complexion and blue eyes common to the Scandinavians settling throughout the West. The professor wasn't sure whether the sheriff's hair had turned white at an early age or was simply so light in color that it looked white. Unlike most westerners, the sheriff seldom wore a hat, so the hair could have been sun-bleached; strangely enough, though, his face wasn't particularly tan despite the lack of a hat and his light complexion. Nothing was remarkable about the sheriff's dress except the fact that he wore his pants so low. As he turned his back toward the professor to wipe grease from his hands, his pants sagged all the way below his butt, leaving the professor unsure how they defied gravity.

'Come to the house for some tea,' the sheriff told the professor as he walked away. As they started toward the back porch of the adobe house, the professor stopped at the sight of a monstrosity of a machine that reminded him of the steam engines that drove riverboats and ocean-going ships, except that it was attached to nothing that he could see.

'Ah, you have an eye for the machines, I see,' the sheriff said. 'I am experimenting, making my own steam engine.'

'For what do you plan to use this?' the professor asked.

'One could use it for many purposes,' the sheriff answered. 'A sawmill, to pump water for irrigation, maybe to replace horses and mules for wagons and plows some day. Pump water to every house and store in town.' The professor noted the way the sheriff's eyes shone as he talked. In his past, the professor had found it necessary to quickly form judgments about people and to put his confidence in those judgments even though he couldn't explain them. He judged the sheriff to be a smart and interesting man. He hoped to have opportunities to form a friendship.

The sheriff's rather pretty wife already had a pot of tea steaming on the table along with some pastries when the two made their way inside. After an introduction she left them alone.

'The discovery of gold can disturb the whole structure of a town,' the sheriff said, the suddenness of the change of subject surprising the professor. He blew across his teacup as his mind raced. The sheriff smiled. 'Ah, Professor, surely you don't think your use of raw gold would go unnoticed in any western town. Devlon and Pitt were startled.'

The professor didn't respond for what seemed to him a considerable time. Finally he simply raised his eyebrows at the sheriff and said nothing.

'New gold is much like a new horse in the pasture or corral,' the sheriff said, taking his time to bite and slowly chew his cookie and follow with some tea.

'A new horse?' the professor asked.

The sheriff poured about half of his cup of tea into his saucer, sat the cup aside, lifted the saucer to his lips, and blew across it. For a minute, the hot tea seemed to be his total focus. Finally, he poured the tea back into his cup, tentatively sipped, nodded his satisfaction, and drank. The professor sipped silently. 'Yes, Professor,' he finally said, 'you know how it is. Every horse in a group knows its place in the pecking order; which drinks first, which chooses its place at the feed trough first, which enters and leaves the gate first. But when a new horse is placed within the group, each horse has to go through the whole process of establishing the pecking order, again, from top to bottom, as if it were an entirely new group of horses thrown together.'

The professor noted that the sheriff's Swedish accent faded when he was talking seriously rather than in short sentences. He smiled slightly, wondering how much of the sheriff's demeanor was an act to throw people off the track of what he was actually trying to accomplish.

'Your gold is like the new horse. Everyone in town must establish his or her position.'

'Does that "everyone" include you, Sheriff?' the professor asked with a slight smile.

'Especially me, Professor. Yah, especially me,' the sheriff said, smiling slightly.

CHAPTER SEVEN

Rusty looked to see that the professor was busy with the younger boys then spat a stream of tobacco into the grass.

'Men who expectorate, do not rate!'

Rusty jumped at the voice and looked around, obviously surprised to find Rachel standing a few feet away. He furrowed his brow trying to figure out what she had said. 'Wha . . .' He caught himself, straightened, and asked, 'Ma'am?'

'Means, if you spit, you ain't—' George Bridges caught himself. His eyes became big as he tried to think how to backtrack. 'It means a gentleman don't spit in public,' he said.

Rachel nodded her agreement, suppressed a grin at the boys, and turned to return to the house. Becky, one of the 7-year-old girls, ran to catch up with Rachel, caught her hand and fell into step with her. 'Come race me, Mrs Hayes,' she urged.

'Why are you so eager to race me?' Rachel asked the child, for whom she had developed an immediate affection. Becky had asked Rachel twice before to race her.

Becky's smile seemed to light her freckled face. 'Because

my mother says she can tell you're a fast woman.'

Rachel managed to catch her tongue before an angry retort slipped out. For several seconds she fought a strong surge of anger, but she also saw her husband watching the younger boys as they played at their morning recess, contentment obvious in his face and demeanor. 'I don't think your mother has seen enough to know that,' Rachel finally said, struggling to keep her anger out of her voice.

'My mama said she might even bet one hundred dollars and her best horse on you,' Becky continued, completely missing Rachel's tension.

'You really shouldn't judge people or horses by appearances,' Rachel managed. She dropped Becky's hand and walked stiffly toward the house.

'Hello Rachel.' She recognized Pitt Hudson's voice immediately.

'Mrs Hayes,' she corrected him. The fact that she felt her ears turn red and knew that he could see her anger made her even more furious. She glanced quickly to confirm that Becky hadn't lingered near her and saw her standing alone by the school.

'My offer is still open, if you're tired of that runty school marm,' he said and nodded toward the professor.

She thought how easy it would be to kick through his knee, the way he was standing with his weight on it, leaning toward her, and how she could follow up with a kick to his groin. She saw more red as the thought flashed through her head, but she also saw her husband looking so content among his students in the schoolyard. 'Stay away from me,' she told Hudson, her voice low with controlled anger.

'Or you'll sic the school marm on me?' he asked sarcastically.

'I don't need anyone else to handle you, unless you jump me from the back,' she answered.

'Guess gold rates right high,' he said, ignoring her threat.

The comment puzzled her, but she glanced again at her husband, and strode away from Hudson toward her house.

Professor Hayes turned in time to see Rachel walking briskly away from Hudson, her back stiff. He walked to meet Hudson halfway as the big man led his horse toward him. 'What do you want?' Hayes asked and realized he had walked closer into Hudson's face than necessary.

'Talk to you about some property,' Hudson answered insolently. 'And ask about a fellow whose been skulking around the mountains and range on a tall, black horse over the last few months.'

'I'm not interested in buying or selling property right now,' the professor answered.

'If that woman gets tiresome, my offer to put her to work is still good,' he said and smiled.

The professor balled his fist, but noticed that Hudson had used his elbow to clear his black coat away from his pistol, rigged low for a fast draw. His own pistol was stuck in his belt behind his back, underneath his long coat. He also heard the children playing in the school yard behind him. From the corner of his eye, he saw several of the older boys edging into the area, coming, he knew to admire Hudson's fine white stallion. Gunplay would clearly endanger his students. 'Not now nor here,' Hayes told him.

'Any time, any place,' Hudson answered. He stared at the professor for a long moment, and finally swung into the saddle.

'Don't come back here,' Hayes told him.

'Why, I'm a public-spirited citizen, and this is public property,' Hudson responded and spurred his horse. As he rode by the older girls gathered near the well, he tipped his hat and made an exaggerated bow from the waist.

'I figured there was more between that woman and Pitt Hudson than met the eye,' Ethlyn Carter said. 'Imagine them visiting right in front of the professor and the children.'

Sarah Crossley, wife of a local barber, nodded knowingly. 'Makes you think there might be something to the rumor that she was one of Hudson's girls someplace else.'

'And that Professor Hayes,' Ethlyn said, 'talking to Pitt Hudson right there in front of the children. And remember all the gold he had that first day he came here? I always figured there was someone else behind Pitt Hudson and his women out there.'

Both shook their head in disapproval.

CHAPTER EIGHT

'You're sure you would rather stay here?' the professor asked Rachel. 'I can rent another horse or horse and buggy.'

'If you're not disappointed that I'm not going with you, I would really love to unpack and set up our new things,' Rachel said.

The Ute boy came around the corner of the school building riding a mustang pony and leading the professor's walking horse, red stallion and new mare as well as a mule with a large pack. 'The boy's good with horses,' the professor said watching him with the horses. 'And I'll be glad to have someone out on our place.'

The small stable and carriage house that came with the teacher's house wasn't large enough for all three horses. He

45

was going to take the boy and horses out to some land he owned a few miles from town, both to get the horses on grazing and to have the boy overlook the site.

'Good morning,' Rachel said to the boy. He simply raised his hand toward them but didn't speak. 'What name do you prefer?' Rachel asked.

'Miners called me Sumbitch Ute,' the boy said.

Rachel's mouth fell open a bit. The professor coughed a bit as he stifled a laugh.

'I work with miners,' the boy told them. 'I speak damn good English. Miners teach me. Goddamn sumbitch. You bastard! You fuck up a wet dream, sumbitch! They teach me heap damn English.'

Rachel and the professor stood silently until the professor cleared his throat. 'I, uh, don't think we can call you Sumbitch Ute.'

The boy sat silent, obviously thinking. 'They call me Ute Bastard, Goddamned Ute sometime,' he finally said.

'Would you get my rifle and scabbard?' the professor asked and pointed toward the carriage house.

'Damn straight, sumbitch Professor,' the boy answered and rode away.

The professor looked toward Rachel, not sure what reaction to expect. She was half-turned away with her face twisted and red. He was sure she was about to burst out crying. Finally, she turned enough to look her husband in the eye, twisted her face up and partially covered it with her hand.

The professor laid his hand gently on her shoulder.

'Goddamned sumbitch professor! Keep your hands to yourself!' she spat at him.

The professor jerked his hand away and tried to think what to say until Rachel burst out laughing so hard she could hardly stand. The professor was shocked, but then laughed with her. They laughed until they were hanging on to each other for support.

'Damn straight ace of spades; Henry fucking forty-four,' Ute told them approvingly as he rode up with the professor's rifle and scabbard in his hand.

Rachel gained enough control to speak before the professor did. 'Is it OK if we simply call you, Ute?'

'Shit-fire and save the matches, good name,' Ute answered.

Rachel turned and walked quickly to the house. 'See you for supper,' she managed to the professor. 'And take good care of my Eva, Ute,' she added.

'Do you have a rifle?' the professor asked Ute as they rode away. 'We'll get you one just like mine on the way through town. We will call it a Henry without the other words.'

An hour and a half later, the professor and Ute pulled up at the entrance to a narrow canyon sided with steep rocky walls. A creek about six feet wide poured through the gap, swirling and dancing over large rocks most of the way but with a couple of deep pools. A few willows and cottonwoods grew along the stream bed. A small spring poured out of the steep rock side of the canyon, about six feet above ground level. About one hundred feet ahead, the canyon twisted, effectively blocking sight beyond the turn. Ute pulled his new Henry from its scabbard and pointed to a spot bare of grass about twenty feet ahead. 'You tracks?' he questioned.

The professor looked for a long moment before he saw dimly imprinted tracks in the bare space. Grass between the tracks and where the two sat their horses showed no sign that he could see. Of course his long-time riding partner in Texas, Arthur L. Schmittzen, had often told him that he couldn't track an elephant through a flower garden, and that his wife, Kathleen, could out track Hayes 'ten ways to Sunday'. After looking over the area between the two of them and the bare earth and tracks, as well as the sides and tops of the canyon walls, the professor rode forward. Ute slid from his horse, keeping his rifle in his hands, and bent over the tracks. After a minute or so, he walked ahead up the canyon, keeping his eyes to the ground except for occasional glances ahead and above. The professor trailed so as not to damage any sign.

'Two, three days,' Ute told the professor. 'In, then back,' he added, showing where a track pointed away from the canyon overlaying the track going into the canyon.

The professor thought silently for a couple of minutes. 'OK, Ute. Keep your eyes peeled.' He pulled his own rifle from its scabbard. Almost immediately he wondered if Ute understood. Ute looked at the professor, saw the doubt in his eyes, and opened one of his eyes widely with his fingers to show that he understood. The professor almost laughed despite the tension.

Ute pointed to wagon tracks, which lay on the other side of the creek and looked back at the professor, a question in his eyes. 'My wagon,' Hayes answered, nodding his head. As they rode ahead, the professor wondered if someone might have followed his wagon tracks into the valley to see who had come in and why. He thought for the first time since the wedding of Angus Gillis mentioning that they might be neighbors. He had been so centered on the wedding that he hadn't thought to ask how Angus knew about his presence in this valley. And, if Angus knew, who else might know?

He felt a prickle on the back of his neck as they rode through the canyon to the valley beyond. The path was easy despite the rugged look of the stone canyon walls. The bottom was grassy with only scattered stones, the path rising in elevation but not steep enough to challenge one on horseback or foot. The few scattered trees were close beside the stream. As the canyon entered the valley, the sides quickly widened and then swung to the side, gradually shrinking as the valley floor rose gently to the canyon edge with the sides eventually no more than ten feet high. As they approached the valley, the professor pointed to an area at the edge of the canyon wall where large boulders were jumbled together. 'A good lookout. You can see in the canyon and miles beyond,' he said, and again watched Ute to see if he comprehended.

Ute nodded again and held his hand above his brow as if shading the sun and looking into the distance. The professor pulled up as soon as they rode into the valley. He looked for any signs of people, but he also stopped almost every time he visited just to appreciate the view. The valley, covered with deep, green grass, ran for more than a mile, rising slightly in elevation until thick forest covered the land. The forest swept up and away for a long distance. The professor knew that where he and Ute sat was the only entrance to the grassy valley or the timberland above. A dozen or so longhorn cattle grazed in the distance along with three horses. Near the cattle, several elk stopped grazing, watched the professor and Ute, and returned, worry free, to their grazing. 'Try to shoot deer or elk outside the valley,' the professor told Ute. 'These will be only for emergency food.'

Ute nodded. 'Some watanka, buffler, too,' he told the professor. 'Drive some in . . .' he seemed to search for a word until he pantomimed driving buffalo into the valley.

The professor nodded. He would never have thought of trying that, but he liked the idea right away. He had thought a great deal about the fact that the buffalo seemed destined to disappear in the wild, probably much faster than most people realized. No sight had more sickened him than coming upon hundreds of buffalo carcasses rotting on the plains down in Texas where hide-hunters had slaughtered them, taken only the hides and allowed so many tons of meat to rot. He and Arthur L., as he referred to his former partner, had talked of how much sense it would make to confine the big beasts to a valley somewhere and raise them for their meat and hide. They had talked of settling on water to control miles of prairie for grazing to protect and manage the buffalo like ranchers did cattle. Of course the fly in the ointment had always been how you would transport the meat. There was no way you could drive buffalo to market as they did cattle. Even if there were a railroad nearby, the only way to get the meat to market would be to dry or salt it. Kathleen had suggested to them that if one did it up in Montana or Canada, you could let the meat freeze and ship it in winter only.

The professor realized that he was woolgathering when he needed to get Ute settled and himself back to Rachel. He started Napoleon toward the small stone cabin he had built. The one room was sixteen by sixteen with a fireplace that drew the smoke moderately well. The floor was still dirt although he planned to lay a stone floor – flagstone, he remembered Kathleen had called it. Or perhaps cut timber and split the logs into halves, smooth side up – puncheon. He was struck by how poor the cabin looked since he now had Rachel. It had been OK for bachelor doings but not nearly as good as what he wanted for Rachel. But, no matter how hard he tried, he couldn't seem to get the building right. Perhaps he could find someone in town to hire, he thought. The piles of stone he had dragged up for future building and the few logs piled behind the cabin looked more like clutter than promise. Hopefully Rachel would be more taken with the beauty of the valley than depressed by the squalor of the house site. They would have the year living in the teacher's house with weekends and holidays to work on improving this site, he reminded himself.

He managed to get his mind back to the present. Ute seemed pleased by what he saw. 'Sleep there,' Ute told him, pointing to the area under the wagon and tossing his blanket roll into the back of the wagon. 'Not like to sleep inside house.' He led the mule to the house, removed the tarp covering the packs, and began to unload the supplies into the house.

While Ute was unloading and storing supplies inside, the professor rode around the point of the canyon wall into the valley and up the steep slope to a tall rock tower reaching above the remainder of the rock. Emotions warred inside him at the sight. The small gold deposit meant a good start for him and Rachel, but the precarious appearance of the leaning rock tower made him shiver every time he looked at it. He turned his attention to the ground around him, pleased to find no sign of anyone riding up to the site.

Ute had unpacked the mule by the time the professor returned to the cabin. He had rubbed down the mule's back with a sack from the supply cache and slapped the beast on the rear to send him toward the pasture. He pointed toward Red and Eva and the valley where the other horses grazed, question in his expression.

'Let's lead them out to the other horses,' the professor said.

Ute nodded, mounted, and led the two thoroughbreds toward the other horses. The professor decided that Ute understood more English than he spoke as he followed. 'Work with these horses when you can,' the professor told him as he pointed to the three horses already in the pasture. 'They've never been ridden. I want them gentled rather than broken,' he said. 'When you have time, drag dead wood down near the cabin for fires. The most important thing is to watch for anyone else coming into the valley, but don't get into a fight with anyone.'

'Damn straight,' Ute answered and patted his new rifle. 'Ute be Johnny on the spot lookout for horses.'

CHAPTER NINE

The next day, A.J. hadn't told Rachel anything except that he was going to town, but she sensed that something was wrong, much like the afternoon he had ridden off to town and fought Curt Tucker, so she felt relieved when she heard a horse stop outside the door. She turned to the stove, pushed the pot of already hot water back on to the eye to boil, and dumped coffee she had ground earlier into the pot. Her husband, she had already learned, was fussy about his coffee. He wanted it boiling hot and strong, but freshly brewed.

She spun around in shock when the door burst open and slammed against the wall. Two men rushed in brandishing pistols. Both had their faces masked with bandannas, and wore their hats pulled low over their faces. 'Where's your husband?' the taller one demanded, his black eyes darting rapidly about the room.

Before Rachel could form any words, the tall man motioned silently for his partner, a shorter but very heavy set man with gray eyes, toward the door to the bedroom. 'No!' Rachel shouted angrily.

Both men stopped and stared at her for a moment, and then looked hard at the door to the other room as if some information had been revealed to them. The tall man moved to the wall on one side of the bedroom door and signaled his partner to enter the room. The short man crouched slightly then bolted through the curtain that blocked off the door, his gun panning the room ready to fire. The tall man waited expectantly, his gun poised and his back pressed to the wall. Finally, the shorter man reappeared. 'He ain't here, Ace,' he said. Even in her fear, Rachel tried to memorize the voices, since she could see so little of their faces. Ace tangled his fingers in Rachel's long hair and twisted her head painfully to the side. 'Why'd you try to stop him?' he asked angrily. 'Answer!' he demanded when Rachel stood mute.

'It's just,' Rachel paused searching for a reasonable sounding answer. 'It's just private in there,' she finally managed.

The shorter man picked up A.J.'s short, double-barreled shotgun from the corner, holstered his pistol and shoved the shotgun's barrels into the hollow of Rachel's neck. 'Where's your husband?' he demanded again in a rasping voice.

Rachel fought to stay on her feet as Ace twisted her head. Color drained from her face, making her few freckles stand out more clearly. 'Town,' was all she could manage.

'Where's he keep the gold?' Ace asked, twisting her head further for emphasis.

In the small coffee pot. He had left a hundred dollars there for her in case of an emergency, she thought, but her resolve stiffened. 'He keeps it with him,' she lied.

Ace jerked her hair harder. Rachel cried out in pain and fear. She noticed a peculiar smell about the tall one. *What was that smell?* It jogged a memory but wasn't clear. It occurred to her how odd it was that she was trying to figure out an obscure odor now, in the midst of this horror.

53

Ace slammed Rachel against the wall next to the stove, just as coffee started boiling on to the stovetop. He picked up a towel and lifted the coffee pot toward Rachel. 'Tongue seems frozen,' he said. His voice sounded like he enjoyed what he was doing. 'Let's thaw it out.'

Rachel tried to pull away but stopped because of the pain when he twisted her hair harder. The pot was just above her eyes, tipping further and further over.

'No,' the shorter man said. Ace stopped at the shorter man's word.

'Deuce, she'll talk,' the tall one argued.

'Later,' Deuce responded. His eyes lighted excitedly. 'I never had no perfessor's fancy wife before.'

He leaned the shotgun against the door, stepped forward, and ran his finger across her cheek and down her neck. 'There'll be time for scalding later.'

Rachel slashed at his eyes with the nails of her right hand. Deuce caught her wrist without turning his eyes away from her and smiled evilly, then slapped her hard across her face with his callused right hand.

At first, Rachel felt little, but then the room began to sway. She tasted her own blood.

'Stand up!' Deuce demanded as he grabbed her shoulders and slammed her roughly back against the wall.

Rachel straightened her legs and willed herself to stay on her feet. Deuce leaned closer. *If this isn't an emergency, A.J., I don't know what the devil is,* she told herself silently. 'In the small coffee pot on the shelf,' she told them.

Deuce's eyes swept the shelf until they stopped on the coffee pot. He released Rachel and turned toward the pot. 'You're getting smarter,' he told her.

Rachel was shocked to see the disappointment in their eyes when Deuce shook five gold double eagles out into his palm. A hundred dollars was several months' wages for a cowhand or a teacher.

The two intruders' eyes met. Deuce pocketed the coins. 'The raw gold, sweetie. Where is it?' he demanded.

'I don't know what you mean,' Rachel told him pleadingly.

Deuce grabbed her cheeks and squeezed viciously, and slammed her back against the wall again. Her head bounced. 'No more games!' he warned.

He took a knife from his belt and pushed it against her neck. 'The raw gold,' he said insistently. 'We know about it.'

The gray-eyed one moved his knife and made a scratch down her neck. It wasn't deep, but she soon felt blood well up and run down her neck. Her temper flared at the thought of her dress getting bloodstained, but she realized that it was foolish and dangerous to anger these men.

'By the scales, over his desk,' Rachel blurted. 'He has some there. The rest stays in his coat.'

Deuce touched the point of the knife between her eyes and pushed lightly, just enough to cause a small point of blood to well up. 'That better be right, Missie McNew,' Deuce threatened, heavy sarcasm in his voice. He glared threateningly for a moment before he moved the knife and crossed to the professor's desk.

'In the little tin,' Rachel coached him.

Deuce looked a moment before he found a small round tin in which fulminate of mercury caps for the professor's navy Colts had come from the store.

He eagerly twisted the cap loose, his eyes gleaming at the gold inside.

'Bring it here,' Ace urged.

Rachel watched their eyes. This was obviously what they wanted, although this gold was worth less than the coins.

'That's it,' Ace told his partner, triumph in his voice.

Deuce's eyes lifted back to Rachel. 'Where's the rest?'

Rachel's heart sank. 'With A.J.,' she replied, though she didn't think they would believe her. Her brain raced desperately, seeking some ploy to get away.

Deuce brought out his belt knife, again. 'There's more,' he insisted.

'This is all we need,' Ace told Deuce.

'Shut up!' Deuce snapped.

Rachel tried to pull away. She jerked her hand back when it touched something scalding hot. She reached back again and grabbed the handle of the coffee pot although it burned her hand. She bunched her muscles and swung the pot toward Deuce, splattering coffee in his face.

Deuce grabbed his face and screamed in agony.

Rachel got both hands on the pot and turned it enough to pour on to Ace's leg. As he jerked back, she grabbed his belt buckle and poured coffee under it. Steam rose.

Ace turned loose of Rachel's hair and tried desperately to hold his pants out away from his groin.

Suddenly, Rachel felt like her head had exploded as she slammed back against the wall and slid slowly toward the floor. As she faded away from consciousness, she saw Deuce drawing back for another punch.

'People coming,' Ace told his partner.

Rachel's world went black.

CHAPTER TEN

'Let us look inside the school,' Curtis Tucker told the professor. 'We'll come up to the house in a minute.'

'Certainly,' Hayes answered and smiled to himself. He

appreciated the visitors allowing Rachel a moment's warning that several people were showing up for coffee and some of the cookies she had been preparing before he went to town. These would be their first visitors, so it would be natural for her to be a bit flustered, Hayes figured. The consideration by the man he had fought only a few days earlier gave Hayes a warm feeling.

'Rachel, we have guests,' he announced as he started through the door.

'Wha . . . Rachel! Rachel?'

His eyes took in the coffeepot on the floor and the smaller coffee pot gone in one brief glimpse of the room. His shotgun also lay in the floor.

Quickly, he knelt by his wife and felt her neck for a pulse. He hesitated for a moment afraid of what he would find. Fearfully, he laid his fingers on her neck, rested them for a moment, then quickly moved them. Hayes stood and stepped toward the door, doing so as Tucker and several others slowly made their way from the school toward the house. 'Doc Ramsey!' A.J. called.

Doc Ramsey read the fear in the professor's voice and rushed forward. 'My bag, Curtis,' he told the big miner by his side, before he went to Rachel.

Only a small amount of blood seeped from the split in her forehead where Deuce's fist had caught her unaware, but the area was already swelling and ugly. Ramsey felt her neck for a pulse then shifted his fingers several times. Hayes' hopes fell. It appeared to him that the doctor had been no more able than he to find a pulse. Ramsey lifted one of Rachel's eyelids, then the other.

'Is she. . . ?' Hayes couldn't finish the thought.

'She's alive,' Ramsey responded without looking. Hayes finally breathed. She was alive, but he could tell from the doctor's face that the situation was grave.

Curt Tucker set Dr Ramsey's black bag beside him. 'Get us some fresh water,' the doc told Hayes.

Tucker rose and started toward the well. 'Let Professor get it, Curt. I need you here,' Doc ordered. 'Let him have something to do to keep him busy,' Doc Ramsey added when A.J. was out the door. Doc Ramsey cupped his hands around Rachel's chin and began to work his fingers up and down the back of her neck.

'Someone hurt Mrs Hayes,' voices repeated to each other outside. The group dispersed and rushed in every direction to see if the villains could be found. In San Juan's four years, no 'decent' woman had ever been the victim of even the slightest crime.

A.J. returned to the room with a pan of water and a white towel. 'She's alive and I can't feel any obvious damage to her neck,' Doc told A.J. 'We won't really know any more until she comes around.'

CHAPTER ELEVEN

'You have what?' Rachel asked, her eyes wide with disbelief.

'I have a . . .' Hayes stopped and restarted. 'We have a gold mine,' he told her.

Rachel sat upright, but sharp pain caused her to stop the sudden movement. 'You really mean that?'

'Don't get too excited,' he told her. 'It isn't a big mine. I think it is a small pocket with the remainder of the vein probably thousands of feet underground. I took out enough to buy land and set aside enough to buy some horses and cattle, good horses and good cattle, and. . . .'

He stopped and remained silent for a long moment, before he started again. 'I'm so used to thinking only of myself. You will have a voice in all this, too,' he told her.

'Go ahead,' she urged him, the excitement obvious on her face.

Her enthusiasm touched him. He explained that he had bought a 'small' land grant from a Spanish family, had mined enough gold to pay for it, and was now working to put away enough to buy a few quality cattle and horses. It would be a small ranch, by New Mexico standards, but he believed that smaller ranches that produced high quality stock would do better in the future than the huge ranches that grazed public range now. Fear for Rachel chilled him. 'Someone knows and wants the gold,' he told her. 'I'm not sure who. That is what the two men who attacked you wanted.'

'How would having your gold help them with the mine?' she asked.

Hayes explained that gold from no two sites is exactly alike unless it has been washed around in a stream enough to remove all traces of the other minerals and its shape rounded. Placer gold, which miners panned from stream bottoms, wasn't easy to identify, he explained, but rough gold just removed from the vein could give significant clues to its location for a person who knew minerals and the local geology. 'I should have told you all of this and taken you to see our place before now,' he told her, 'but I thought, foolishly, that not knowing would protect you. We will go when you are well enough. It will be our home if you like it as much as I. And that is where Ute has Red and Eva and a few more horses.'

'Two days,' she told him excitedly. 'Two days and I'll be ready to go.' Professor Hayes didn't believe she would be ready in two days, but he didn't argue.

*

The roan mare stretched its neck to take the piece of dried apple Rachel offered. Her lips took the apple then she snuffled for more. 'That's it,' Rachel told the mare and chuckled.

'Like her?' the professor asked.

'She's wonderful,' Rachel told him.

'She's yours,' he reminded.

Rachel's eyes glowed with delight. The mare reached her nose toward Rachel's face. He started to tell her the mare wouldn't bite, but then remembered how his stallion had reacted to her and realized he didn't have to tell her much of anything about horses. Rachel exhaled lightly into the mare's nostrils. The mare shared breath with Rachel for a long moment then finally laid her chin on Rachel's shoulder.

'You took long enough getting friendly with her,' the professor teased.

'I've always gotten along well with horses and mules,' she told him.

Hayes sobered. 'Are you certain you're up to this trip? It's only been two days since—'

'I said two days and I meant two days,' she said a bit sharply.

Professor Hayes turned Napoleon into the narrow canyon that was the first gap in the stone wall they rode beside, thinking again that Rachel surprised him by being ready to ride only two days after the attack. The floor of the canyon slanted sharply upward and the canyon narrowed to no more than one hundred feet. The apparent increasing altitude of the mesa was borne out by the presence of fir trees instead of the pinon, which topped most of the mesas nearer San Juan. A few patches of white aspen trunks began to appear on the outer edges of the canyon. Cottonwoods began to be replaced by firs along the sides of the clear, bubbling creek that ran through the bottom of the canyon.

A bull elk, almost as large as their horses, snorted and trotted into the aspen, swinging his big rack of antlers side to side. Ahead the canyon narrowed to a neck of no more than fifty feet. Only a few willows grew beside the stream; a thick carpet of grass reached halfway up the horses' legs.

Professor Hayes had stopped looking to see if Rachel was managing to stay with him. She rode like a Comanche, he had decided, as if instinct guided her subconsciously. He cast another look at the large packet of food she had tied behind her saddle. The smell of fried chicken had been playing havoc with his appetite the whole time they had been riding.

'Sure you're not too hungry?' he asked. 'We could picnic anywhere along here.'

She chuckled. 'You'll have to—'

Shards of stone flew from the wall of rock. One piece glanced off the professor's hat. Dirt kicked up in front of their horses. The sound rang down the narrow canyon and echoed.

Hayes turned to yank Rachel to the ground but found her gone. He felt like his heart had stopped until he saw her rolling swiftly toward an outcropping of rock, and then scramble on her hands and feet. He grabbed his rifle from his scabbard, turned Napoleon sideways, and bailed off to join his wife.

Pounding hoofs raced down the canyon toward them. Hayes glanced to confirm that Rachel was uninjured as he raised his rifle, eared back the hammer, and squeezed the slack from the trigger, ready to fire as soon as the attacker appeared in his sights.

'Professor! No shoot, sumbitch Professor!' a high-pitched voice called. 'Ute,' the voice added.

Hayes eased the pressure he had begun to apply to the trigger, but kept his rifle up and ready. Ute raced around the bend on a black mare, his hair and the horse's mane flying. Hayes watched carefully to see that no one was pursuing Ute and raised his rifle muzzle skyward, but kept his finger on the trigger and his thumb on the hammer.

'No recognize,' Ute said excitedly as he pulled the mare to a skidding stop. 'Miss Rachel?' he asked, his fear plain on his face until Rachel stood, obviously unhurt.

The professor followed Ute's eyes to Rachel and remembered the sight of her scrambling desperately behind the rock right after the shot ricocheted down the valley. 'What the. . . !' he caught himself then lost it again. 'You crazy. . . !'

'I'm OK,' Rachel assured him and laid her hand on his arm. He caught himself just before he shrugged her hand away.

'I thought you the ones who shooting at me,' Ute explained.

White streaks were obvious against the gray rocks from which the professor had erected walls of the cabin. His eyes swung to the small tipi Ute had built for himself between the walls and the small spring a short way downslope.

The horses! It struck the professor that the horses were nowhere in sight.

'In hollow,' Ute quickly volunteered, reading the professor's eyes.

Hayes swung his eyes in the direction that Ute nodded and saw a fence erected by dragging treetops and limbs into place, effectively blocking off a deep hollow that made its way into a shallow side canyon into the mesa. One of several small springs he had found in the valley was there, he remembered. And from above the hollow a rifleman could cover the trail through which they had entered the canyon.

'Riflemen shoot at me, horses,' Ute explained when he

saw that the professor understood. 'Aiyee! I happy I only shoot to scare you away,' Ute said. 'Then recognize horse and Miss Rachel's hair.'

Hayes cast his eyes toward Rachel, but she wasn't listening. Her eyes swept the valley and her mood seemed distant. Ute shifted his eyes to her, also. Finally Rachel seemed to remember they were there. Her attention swung back to them. 'Is this really yours?' she asked.

'Ours,' Hayes reminded her. 'Ours!'

'It is the most beautiful place I've ever seen,' she said and squeezed his arm.

Hayes looked again, remembering his reaction the first time he'd ridden in and seen this valley almost hidden, surrounded by the mesa except for the narrow entrance. The valley ran more than two miles long and varied from a few hundred yards to a half mile wide. Rock walls, mostly red but with streaks of gray, ranged from one hundred feet to less than ten feet high. The steepness of the walls varied, but the slope everywhere looked to be too steep for livestock to climb in or out. Most of the valley was meadow with grass knee deep to people. Two small streams ran through the valley, joined one hundred feet in front of the house, and then ran out of the valley through the canyon they had followed into the valley. A few trees, mostly willow and cottonwood, were scattered along the streams. One area of about five acres was a mass of head-high willows and marked what the professor knew to be a series of beaver ponds and runs, thickly populated by cutthroat trout and whitefish. One corner of the valley was heavily timbered, mostly fir but with a band of white-trunked aspen surrounding it. As one went higher, fir stretched into the distance.

Hayes spoke softly as Rachel took in the valley. 'I bought the valley and mesa surrounding it, about seven and a half thousand acres. We'll ride to the mine after lunch. You need to know about it . . . in case. And when we get back I'll show you the deed and my will.'

Her eyes revealed her distress at this tack of the conversation, but her practical side took over and she nodded.

'I built this cabin before I met you,' he told her. 'I'll level this and start over if you'd rather—'

'It's perfect,' she said. 'I'll do a garden and run water from the spring.' She nodded toward a flat area near the rill that ran off from the small spring near the house site.

'I'll hire some help to finish the house,' the professor told her. 'It's a long way from people,' he added, watching her for response. She showed no concern.

'Hattie and Angus Gillis have a place backed up to the mesa outside the valley,' he said. 'They are the nearest neighbors.' Hayes had figured that out after the wedding and still wondered how they had known about his buying the valley.

'There's no one I'd rather have,' she said contentedly.

The professor took her elbow and led her around the corner of the cabin to where a square perhaps eight feet wide and twelve feet long had been dug up and a scattering of plants were peeking through the soil. Rachel walked and bent by the plot, picked up some of the loose soil, looked at it, smelled it, squeezed some in her hand, and inspected it again. 'The soil looks good,' she said. 'The plants aren't large enough to identify.'

'Flowers, so far,' he told her. 'They're not planted in any particular order. I was in a hurry to get them into the ground and raise them for seed for this year. Most of them came from Kathleen Schmittzen, the wife of my ranger partner, Arthur L. Schmittzen. And a few are ones I've picked up and saved over the years when I saw something I liked, mostly from Texas.'

'Flowers do almost as much to make a house a home as the smell of bread baking,' Rachel said. She stood, took the professor's arm in her hands, and hugged closely to him, kissing him on his cheek.

'There are phlox, bachelor button, coneflower, blue bonnets, Indian paint brush. I'm not sure exactly what it all is.' He pointed to the edge of the spring where a ceramic pot stood. 'Some rose cuttings I'm trying to root. Some Iris that was common around Texas homesteads.'

Every day seemed to reveal parts of her husband that Rachel liked . . . loved, she told herself. She turned to face him and hugged him tightly. 'I believe I could use a nap inside our cabin,' she told him as she nuzzled against his neck. 'Don't you think Ute should go back up on the ridge to watch for anyone that might be attracted to the shooting?' she asked. 'I wouldn't want our nap interrupted.'

Rachel was amused to see some pink as the professor blushed, but he returned her hug. 'I think that could be arranged,' he told her and walked toward Ute.

Rachel tugged the blanket roll behind her saddle loose and walked into the house, warm pleasure flushing her as well. She had read of people using champagne to christen ships. She supposed they'd just have to christen the cabin in the best way available.

'It gives me the heebie-jeebies,' Rachel said and shuddered as she looked at the narrow chimney of rock and the shaky-looking ladder the professor had used to extract the gold. Piles of shattered gray rock lay to the side. The professor's tools lay neatly on a stone shelf sheltered from weather by a ledge.

'How do you work up there?' she asked.

'Very carefully,' Hayes answered. 'The vein is rotten and not large. An up-thrusting of quartz exposed to the weather for centuries, probably.'

He shook his head. 'Whoever tried to force information from you would be very disappointed if they realized how little there is left. With very hard work, we might get out enough to stock up with a few good horses and cattle, and perhaps a little reserve.'

'I can't imagine wanting more,' Rachel said as she walked back to where she could see the sweep of the valley. 'Except, perhaps, children.'

CHAPTER TWELVE

Professor Hayes scraped the bit of red mud off of his boot on the edge of the first step in front of San Juan's one church. Rachel's fingers tightened nervously on her husband's arm.

'Have thine own way, Lord. Have thine own way.
Thou art the potter, I am the clay.'

'More enthusiasm than harmony,' Hayes told her lightly, nodding toward the source of the singing inside the church. They paused inside the door. A few heads turned toward the latecomers, but most remained fixed on their open song-books. An insistently waving hand near the front of the congregation caught Hayes' eye. It took him a moment to recognize the man dressed in a neat brown suit, a white shirt, and tie. Curt Tucker waved his oversized, hairy hand toward the empty space in the pew beside himself and Rusty.

Rachel looked uncertainly toward her husband. Hayes

hung his hat on one of the wooden pegs beside the door and strode forward. He wondered if the redness of the miner's face was due to the warmth of the crowded room or from scrubbing in hot water, and smiled at the thought. Tucker shook hands enthusiastically with the professor and then engulfed Rachel's hand. *I bet he could strike a match on these*, Rachel thought as his heavily callused hands took hers. The grace and gentleness he showed, however, surprised her. Equally surprising to her was the affection she saw in her husband's face as he nodded and spoke to the miner. This was the man he had fought in the street a few days earlier, Rachel thought, and shook her head at the ways of men.

Tucker elbowed his son. Rusty looked at his father, question in his expression. The big miner nodded toward the professor and Rachel. Rusty looked at the two and back at his father, obviously still uncertain what was expected. Tucker nodded more insistently. This time, Rusty took the cue and nodded politely if unenthusiastically. 'Good morning, Professor. Mrs Hayes.' The miner beamed approvingly at his son. The professor nodded to Rusty and leaned toward his father. 'Rusty has a fine mind and the instincts of a gentleman,' Hayes told him. Tucker appeared to be even more proud. Rusty relaxed visibly when he heard the professor's remarks.

Professor Hayes smiled to himself as he thought how much the appearance and demeanor of the boy had changed since the first day of school. The pressure of Rachel's hand on his arm drew his attention away from these thoughts. Hattie Gillis stood in the front of the church where she had been directing the singing and motioned Rachel forward. Finally, it soaked through to him that the song was over. Other faces, most of which Hayes didn't recognize, turned expectantly toward Rachel. Hattie motioned Rachel forward again, this time more vigorously, and nodded toward the organ. 'Do you play?' the professor asked Rachel.

Rachel nodded.

'Play well?' he asked.

She hesitated for a moment and nodded again.

'Then go,' he whispered. 'Sounds to me like they need you.'

Angus Gillis stepped forward and pulled the pump organ away from the wall and placed the bench, its seat slanted toward the keyboard, in front of Rachel. Rachel hesitated by the organ for a moment, running her fingers over the oak wood. Her face flushed deep red. Hayes admired his wife's proud, erect posture. The blue velvet of her dress, which she had quickly but lovingly sewn, reminded him of the blue bonnets that covered the prairies every spring in his native Texas. His new wife, Hayes thought admiringly, was a woman who would be even prettier ten years and twenty years from now. Fire burned in his belly again when her face turned so that he could see the discoloration left where the two men looking for his gold had struck her.

Rachel sat on the bench and lovingly ran her fingers along the wood before lifting the cover from the keys. She pumped the pedals. Her face seemed to glow with joy.

At that moment, the professor decided that Rachel would have a pump organ that Christmas regardless of price or difficulties of delivery.

Mumbling in the congregation intruded upon his thoughts. Brother Johnnie appeared to be distinctly uncomfortable standing beside the pulpit. Even the nicest suit of clothes in the building, other than that of the professor, didn't keep him from a scarecrow-like ungainliness. The clerical collar looked ostentatious in a non-denominational frontier church, the professor thought, but then he admitted to himself that he wouldn't have liked Brother Johnnie no matter what he wore.

'Number eighty-six,' Hattie announced. '*Bringing in the Sheaves.*' She seemed as happy to have Rachel play as Rachel herself was.

Rachel opened a songbook, pressed it flat, and moved the sliding wooden clips to hold it in place. She took a deep breath and began the opening chords. Her fingers slid knowingly and affectionately across the keys. Hattie began the singing in a pure soprano while enthusiastically lining out the music with her left hand. Her face beamed with pleasure. The professor paid more attention to the organ than to the singing. Rachel did play well, he agreed to himself, quite well, indeed.

The pure tenor voice of Curt Tucker grabbed his attention, both for its beautiful, clear tone and the surprise at such a tenor coming forth from such a large, rough-skinned man. Rusty sang in a much lower baritone, but also skillfully. But the volume from the congregation was much less than he expected. Awe and fascination at Rachel's playing, he figured. He turned to look at the faces in the congregation.

Realization chilled him like a blue norther on the Staked Plains. Most members of the congregation stood with mute disapproval on their faces. Several sent sharp glances first to Rachel and then to him; several closed their hymnals as the professor watched.

He looked sharply toward Rachel. She was so enthralled in the organ that she seemed unaware of the singing. Hattie sang more loudly as her eyes slung darts at those not singing. Several resumed singing, although half-heartedly. Most stared ahead, stonily silent. Some who had sung from the beginning increased their volume to make up the difference, but it became obvious that few were singing. As

Rachel played the last verse, she looked toward the congregation and appeared to be puzzled at the diminishing volume. One strong bass voice continued enthusiastically until the end of the song. The professor turned to find the singer. Devlon Gibson nodded cordially to him.

Rachel returned to her seat for what seemed to Hayes to be a rather insipid sermon with little Biblical content nor stirring delivery. To be fair, he also recognized that he probably wouldn't have appreciated the Sermon on the Mount, had Brother Johnnie delivered it. The professor had the impression that the congregation's hostility hadn't sunk in on Rachel as she played. He debated with himself whether or not to bring it to her attention but finally decided not to do so. She could reach her own conclusions without his help.

Brother Johnnie concluded his sermon and signaled Hattie Gillis that it was time to lead the final hymn. She walked to the front and waved for Rachel to come to the organ again. 'We'll close with number forty-eight, *What A Friend We Have In Jesus*,' Hattie announced.

Brother Johnnie became aware of the angry stares from many in the congregation. Rachel stayed in her seat and did not return to the organ. Hayes felt tension as sharply as if it were a physical squeeze on him. 'Rachel,' Hattie said firmly and nodded toward the organ, 'if you will, please.'

Rachel hesitated another moment before she moved to the organ. She settled, turned to the page and fixed the place. Her eyes swept the congregation. Professor Hayes saw her back stiffen in response to the obvious disapproval by so many. Hattie nodded to Rachel to begin. At the end of the introductory bars, Brother Johnnie interrupted loudly. 'Bow for the benediction,' he directed and extended his arms to pray.

Rachel stopped in mid-bar. The next note came from Hattie's mouth and then she stopped in shock. Only Devlon

Gibson's deep bass continued for a full line. Brother Johnnie's hands remained extended. 'May the Lord bless you and keep you and give you peace. Amen,' he intoned.

Everyone sat in shocked silence for a moment then seemed to stir at the same time. They gathered Bibles and parasols, replaced hymnals in the racks, any kind of activity to try to escape the embarrassing moment. Rachel sat frozen in apparent disbelief for a moment and then ran her fingers down the keyboard, lovingly caressing the ivory. She carefully lowered the cover over the organ keys, placed the stool against the organ, and stepped to the professor's side. Red suffused her neck and then her face, but her lips were pressed together so tightly that bloodless white outlined them. She said nothing but clasped A.J.'s hand between her elbow and her side, and stepped firmly toward the exit. A few people looked sympathetic but said nothing. A few stopped to speak kindly to the professor and Rachel who rewarded each with a sincere thank you.

People parted for Devlon Gibson. Anger welled up in Hayes as the big man parked himself in front of them, causing them to stop. It was evident to the professor that Rachel wanted to get away as quickly as possible. He turned his best killer glare on the big man, but it was wasted. All of Gibson's attention was on Rachel.

'You play beautifully, Mrs Hayes,' he told her as he took her hand in his. 'I enjoyed it very much.'

It seemed to the professor that Gibson's eyes lingered on Rachel's shape longer than necessary. 'But you are going to create a problem for me,' Gibson added.

Rachel's eyes flicked quickly to her husband then back to Gibson.

'You look so lovely in that blue velvet that every woman in one hundred miles will want to order some.' He paused long enough for the words to be savored. 'There is no way

71

of getting so much blue velvet. And besides, it will not look nearly as good on anyone else.'

He turned his eyes to the professor and offered his hand. Briefly the professor was in a quandary. Would it be two-faced to shake this man's hand as if he liked him, and as if he didn't object to the way he looked at his wife? Or would it be boorishly uncivil to refuse to simply shake a man's hand? Reluctantly he took the huge hand, carefully gripping it in such a way as to keep the big man from crushing his much smaller hand. Devlon Gibson squeezed briefly but stopped as he realized Hayes was again prepared. He smirked lightly and touched his hat. 'Mrs Hayes,' he said. 'Professor.' He was gone.

The man really irritated Hayes. He didn't want to like him, yet he had been very courteous to Rachel in the face of others being so cruel. He quickly guided Rachel through the crowd and strode beside her toward the school and their house. A sideward glance showed Rachel trying to blink away tears. He could think of nothing to say. He was sure he'd never felt more distressed in his life. He could quote dozens of poets, practically any voice from the Greek classics that anyone could name, Shakespeare and the Bible, yet he couldn't make one word of comfort come forth for his wife.

CHAPTER THIRTEEN

'I'm sorry,' Devlon Gibson told the professor.

The only thing that surprised Professor Hayes was that he cared as much as he did. He had only taken the teaching job originally to become known and to establish some local credibility in case the title to the land he had bought was challenged. As it turned out, the title to the land seemed solid now. His original purpose had been met, but he felt a deep sense of loss that he wasn't going to be allowed to complete the year as his students' teacher.

'I know what you're thinking,' Gibson told the professor. 'Everyone thinks that I control the vote of the School Board and that's usually true,' he admitted. 'I can almost always persuade the men or browbeat them or bribe them or do something to get my way, but I can't persuade their wives.'

Hayes stared silently at Gibson. 'I doubt if any of the men think you should be fired,' Gibson continued, 'but their wives do. End of argument.'

'The decision is final and immediate?' Hayes asked.

Gibson nodded. 'The house is yours for the rest of the month.' He paused and then slammed his hand down hard on his desk. 'I hate this!' he exclaimed. 'We didn't get off on a good footing, Professor, but I respect you.'

'Mr Gibson,' Hayes said, touched the brim of his hat and left.

'Tell your students you will teach them in our home whenever it is safe,' Rachel told Hayes.

'This is actually for the best,' he told her. 'I'm a crippled up old former Texas Ranger, which is another way to say gunfighter.'

'You have a God-given talent,' Rachel told him as she squeezed his hand. 'You should use it.'

'They have given us the remainder of the month in this house,' Hayes told her and squeezed her hand back. 'I'm going to have to find help to work the land, finish the building and to defend the place.'

Rachel dropped his hand and shook her head in disagreement of what she knew was coming. 'You'll be safer here,' he argued.

'Ute and I will hold the place,' she said. 'And I can do a world toward setting up housekeeping.'

'But—'

'But nothing,' she interrupted and grinned. 'Do you forget that I got on a train and rode all the way out here to have my own home? I apologize if I cause you more worry, but I am not staying here.'

The professor realized that any argument he made was wasted. And, truth be told, he didn't blame her. 'Didn't know what you were letting yourself in for when you stepped forward at the depot, did you?' she asked playfully.

'If I had, I would have stepped forward more quickly,' he said.

CHAPTER FOURTEEN

The organ music froze the professor in his steps. It took longer for the one strong voice and several half-hearted ones singing *Bringing in the Sheaves* to penetrate his consciousness. Flickering light from open flames near the end of the one street in Brazos Christos cast an eerie light upon the scene. The weaker voices faded out, leaving only the one strong voice to complete the song. Upon the last chord of the hymn, the voice switched immediately into a loud message of fire and brimstone. A short, round-shouldered man in a bright blue, swallow-tailed coat pounded his fist and described the ever burning torture of perdition for sinners who didn't repent and made it clear that all present were sure to be included among that number.

The professor remained out of sight in the shadows at the back of the small gathering. Two rough-looking men whose dress identified them as miners elbowed each other and laughed at the preacher's efforts, their voices competing with that of the preacher. The preacher paid them no attention other than to raise his voice ever louder. After several minutes he lifted his hands, bowed his head, and prayed loudly. The scoffers didn't stop even for the prayer. The only acknowledgment the preacher made of the two was to direct one eye toward them. Finally, he concluded with a long amen and extended his hat. 'The work of the Lord takes money, brothers and sisters,' he intoned. 'Many hands make light work. Even the widow gave Christ her mite. All donations will be appreciated.'

A small boy passed the preacher's hat among the crowd. When the preacher received it back empty, his face twisted in anger. 'I asked you to dig down for the Lord and you shunned him. Brethren and sisters,' he proclaimed in his sermon voice, 'the Lord says that to those much has been given, much will be expected. You might not feel wealthy, but tonight you will eat a full supper and go to bed under a dry, warm roof. To so many who are extremely blessed, I ask that you now contribute to the spreading of the Gospel to the lost.' He handed his hat back to the boy and nodded for him to go through the crowd again. While the lad passed the hat, the preacher sat playing the organ and sang *How Sweet Thou Art* in a deep and reverent voice. Most in the crowd enthusiastically joined in. When the boy returned and they completed the first verse, he looked into the hat expectantly. His eyes narrowed; he looked distressed.

'I beseech you to heed the words of the Lord. Render to

Caesar that which is Caesar's and render unto to the Lord that which is the Lord's. Look into your hearts and pocketbooks and give generously as the Lord has given generously to you.' Again the boy returned with an empty hat. When the preacher looked up from the empty hat, a number of watchers tittered. The rowdy miners guffawed. The preacher's face glowered in near rage. 'I asked you dig deep and you gave nought. I asked you to emulate the dear widow who gave her mite and you turned a deaf ear. And, finally, I've asked you to render unto God as you render unto Caesar as well as your baser tastes, and you send the Lord's treasury back empty.' His eyes burned at one and another in the gathering but settled back on the ruffians who had been talking during his sermon and prayer. 'Now you can all go straight to hell!'

The two miners who had been the most inconsiderate began to grumble among themselves while everyone else stood in shocked silence. Finally the two walked toward the preacher. Everyone scurried aside to clear a path to the preacher's little platform. The preacher stood his ground facing the men, each of whom was much larger than he. The largest man grasped the lapels of the preacher's frock coat and lifted him so that only his toes touched the ground. 'You telling me to go to the devil?' he asked the preacher and shook him.

'I'm only the tongue of the Lord, heathen,' he responded although his eyes were wide with fear.

The big man stood still for a long moment, then closed his other hand around the preacher's throat. 'We'll see whether it's the Lord or the preacher who croaks,' he said. The other ruffian drew and cocked his pistol. The preacher's eyes turned toward the gun; the gunman rubbed the pistol muzzle across the preacher's nose, and then quickly tilted and fired. One of the flaming torches lighting the scene exploded and blinked out.

The preacher jerked. The big man shook the preacher by the throat and released him. The preacher gasped to get his breath back, then croaked, 'You can throttle this man, but you can't silence the word of the Lord. I'll receive my reward in the glory of heaven and you'll fry forever in brimstone!'

The gunman tilted the pistol toward the preacher's pump organ. Hayes stepped quickly into the light. 'Hold it!' he ordered sharply. The two ruffians and the preacher jerked their heads toward Hayes. 'Turn and you better be using that pistol,' he told the man with the drawn gun. The man froze and turned only his eyes toward the professor. The professor stood with his coat pushed behind his pistol and holster, his fingers hanging only inches from his holstered gun, relaxed but ready.

The two men stared at Hayes for what seemed a long time, and then smiled slightly at the same time. The man who had held the preacher eased his hand closer toward the pistol stuck under his belt.

'You're out of your jurisdiction, aren't you, Ranger Hayes,' a voice said from the dark. 'This isn't Texas.'

The two men froze. 'Ranger?' the one with his gun drawn asked.

Hayes shook his head no.

'Texas Ranger Andrew Jackson Hayes,' the voice from the dark volunteered. Hayes' eyes never left the two men on the platform although he was busy fixing the location of the voice in his mind.

'Not anymore,' Hayes finally volunteered. 'This is strictly private business.'

'Where is this any of your business?' the man with the drawn gun asked, careful not to turn his gun toward the professor.

'I want to buy that organ you were about to shoot,' the professor replied. 'Twenty dollars?' he asked the preacher.

'I don't want to s—' the preacher began, looked back toward the two ruffians and spoke again. 'I only sell the organ if I go with it.'

Hayes took a twenty dollar gold piece from his coat pocket with his left hand and flipped it on to the podium, the clatter of the coin loud in the silence. 'I'd take it most unkindly if you shot my organ,' he told the two men. 'Or my organist,' he added.

The gunman glared at Hayes for a moment, seemed to shrink and dropped the gun into his holster. 'Another time,' the bigger man told the preacher and walked away. The gunman followed.

The preacher straightened his collar, stood erect and shook himself like a rooster fluffing its feathers. As if he suddenly remembered, he quickly dipped and grabbed Hayes' gold piece.

'Xavier, I believe?' Hayes asked as he turned toward the shadow from which the voice had come.

A tall man stepped from the shadow into the flickering light. '*Oui, Monsieur* Ranger.'

The man was much taller than Hayes, but slender, his hair black, his features finely chiseled. 'Xavier David,' Hayes told the preacher without taking his eyes off the man. 'Spelled like David in the Bible but pronounced Da-veed.'

Hayes and David looked each other over for a long moment. Both kept hands relaxed but not far from their pistol grips. 'I'm not a ranger anymore,' Hayes told David.

'*Oui.* I understand you are now Le Professeur Hayes. *Le professeur et mineur* or professor and gold miner,' David translated and cast his eyes toward the preacher.

The preacher's eyes took on a very calculating look.

'Have you any experience as a miner?' Hayes asked the

Frenchman.

'*Mais oui*. Certainly,' David answered. 'But I don't work for wages.'

'It's a small gold deposit,' Hayes told him. 'Ten per cent of the gold we get out within the next three months. Might have to fight, also.'

David's eyes enlarged slightly. 'Another five per cent if I have to use my gun,' David countered.

Professor Hayes hesitated slightly then nodded acceptance.

'Might be interesting to fight on the same side as you,' David said.

'Fifteen per cent for me, too, if I fight,' the preacher said.

'Xavier is a pro,' Hayes responded.

'I'm not a pro,' the preacher said, 'but . . .' his hand flashed and a derringer appeared as if by magic. Hayes was shocked. 'And,' the preacher said as his other hand grabbed a shotgun from underneath his organ seat.

'You help dig gold, you fight if necessary, and you preach, for ten per cent,' the professor answered.

'I don't really believe—' the preacher began.

'I don't care what you believe, so long as my wife gets her organ and a church service in which to play it,' Hayes interrupted tersely.

'I don't believe I have any better offers at the moment,' the preacher said and extended his hand. 'Tolliver. Reverend Oliver Justice Tolliver, at your service.'

CHAPTER FIFTEEN

Hayes stopped Napoleon and stared at his house. A large buckskin stood ground-hitched at the corner; Devlon Gibson's massive frame sat on a pile of building stone while Rachel stood talking to him. Suddenly, Rachel straightened and waved enthusiastically. Gibson turned in such a way that it was obvious that he was already aware of Hayes and his little procession. 'And what does that big fellow get?' David asked.

Hayes ignored David and led his procession forward again.

Gibson continued to talk and smile at Rachel as Hayes approached. Rachel rushed to meet Hayes, but stopped when she saw the dark look on his face. 'What do you want?' Hayes asked Gibson.

'And good day to you, too, Professor,' Gibson responded and continued to smile.

'Don't call me Professor,' Hayes replied sternly.

'I'm here to make an offer,' Gibson told him. 'For your valley,' he added when Hayes didn't answer. 'I'm prepared to offer—'

'No,' Hayes interrupted.

'Maybe we should listen to his listen,' Preacher Tolliver offered.

'You don't have a vote,' Hayes told the preacher without looking at him. He cut his eyes at Xavier. The Frenchman shrugged his shoulders nonchalantly.

'I presume you got your gold here,' Gibson offered, 'but it is the water I need. When you control this valley, you control the water and grazing for miles around.'

'No,' Hayes repeated.

Gibson shrugged his shoulders. 'At least you don't own the land right outside the canyon, do you?'

Hayes stiffened. That plot was like a cork in the neck and his valley the bottle.

'I do,' Xavier said.

Hayes and Gibson turned toward Xavier, surprise equally evident in both faces.

'One hundred sixty acres, filed on all proper and legal like,' Xavier told them and pulled his coat open to show a folded document in his inside pocket. 'It isn't for sale, either.'

Gibson stood and offered his hand to Rachel. 'It was pleasant to visit with you,' he told her. 'And the offer to buy stands, for either,' he told Xavier and Hayes.

'What do you want for it?' Hayes asked Xavier, his voice hard with anger after Gibson was gone.

'As I said, *mon ami*, it isn't for sale,' he replied.

'I'm not your friend, and why do you want the land?' Hayes snapped.

'Ah Professeur, you are so suspicious,' Xavier told him and smiled. 'To raise alfalfa. I will irrigate from the creek and grow alfalfa to sell to ranchers. Perhaps you will buy?' he asked playfully.

'Where's Ute?' Hayes asked Rachel, his voice still hard.

'Here, Professor,' Ute answered. All looked toward the voice and saw Ute behind a stack of building stone, his rifle trained on Xavier and the preacher. Hayes looked pleased for the first time since his arrival.

'Put your stuff over there,' Hayes told Xavier and the preacher and pointed with his head. 'One of us will be on guard at the pass all of the time. Start mining in the morning.'

81

'Hello to you, too, Andrew,' Rachel told him and stalked away toward the completed portion of the house.

CHAPTER SIXTEEN

'*Mon Dieu!*' Xavier swore softly and crossed himself.

'God help us!' Preacher Tolliver declared, equally startled, as they stared at the rotten quartz vein the professor had been working. Even without knowing any geology, the seams of stone, different from the rest of the rock cliff, stood out in obvious relief. Equally obvious were seams and pockets of gold within the quartz. The whole narrow shaft of stone jutting from the remainder of the cliff leaned outward from the cliff with broken seams obvious where the shaft extruded. Near the bottom of the shaft, the seam of quartz and gold widened into a pocket where seams of gold scattered about ten feet wide then halted above ground level. Removal of ore to that point had left an undercutting of the whole rock face, which already leaned outward.

'Since I'm inexperienced in this type work, perhaps it would be better for me to spend all my time praying for those of you working this,' Tolliver opined. 'I'd do that for only five per cent of the gold,' he added.

Hayes and David snorted derisively at Tolliver's words.

'You sure as Hades need all of the praying you can get,' Tolliver protested.

'You been doing this by yourself?' Xavier asked.

'You're crazier than a mule-kicked dog!' Tolliver told him.

'I wouldn't have offered to pay a percentage if getting the

gold out was all peaches and cream,' Professor Hayes told them. 'You can see it for yourselves. Most of the gold that is left is down in this pocket at the bottom, but I don't know how much I can whittle on that pocket without the whole shooting match coming down on top of my head. Still sure you want in on this gold?' the professor asked with a smirk.

'There has to be a better way to get the gold out,' Preacher Tolliver said.

All cast their eyes up and down the cliff face, deeply undercut by the excavation that the professor had already done. A ladder of about ten feet leaned against the side of the undercut section and beneath the overhang. 'As bad as it looks from down here,' the professor admitted, 'it looks worse from the ladder.'

'Can't you blast the whole thing down and extract it?' the preacher asked.

'There is no indication that the vein goes any higher or much deeper underground,' the professor told them. What we have here is a limited pocket. Rich, jewelry-type stuff in rotten quartz but just a pocket. You'd bury the gold under a mountain of debris.'

'When this starts to collapse,' Xavier mused, 'it will likely come down in a hurry. Person on the ladder will have to get down and run to get away. Can't tell exactly which way it might fall or how far.'

'Don't mines use heavy equipment, sluices, that sort of stuff?' the preacher asked.

'Costs a lot of money, perhaps more than the value of the gold left,' the professor replied. 'Besides, that would cause all sorts of runoff and pollute the creek below.'

'Mining makes a mess but this could be a lot of money,' the preacher argued.

'Rachel has a strong opinion: given a choice of more gold or clean water in the creek, she'll take the water. And

I agree,' the professor explained.

Xavier nodded but said nothing.

'Notice I keep the ground under and around the cut clear of debris,' the professor told them. 'Rock taken down needs to be hauled out to the pile,' he added and pointed to several piles of rock. 'There always needs to be at least one person mucking out when someone is on the ladder with the pick. No exceptions and no shortcuts! When that overhang starts to collapse, and it will, it'll be hard enough to get down and away without having to watch where you put your feet.'

'No argument here,' Xavier agreed.

'What about the redskin boy?' the preacher asked and pointed to Ute where he sat atop the ridge on one boulder surrounded by craggy rock above, rifle in his hand.

The professor shook his head. 'He is absolutely forbidden to be down here where we are. He's very mature for his years, but a boy nevertheless. Besides, his job is to be lookout. He has the best eyes I've ever seen. He can see anyone approaching for miles in any direction.'

'Or,' Xavier added with a slight smile, 'anything that goes on down here.'

'True,' the professor agreed with a smile.

'No high grading,' Xavier said.

'High grading?' the preacher asked.

'Slipping chunks of gold or high grade ore into your pockets or whatever and squirreling it away for yourself,' Xavier added. 'Any mining camp I've ever seen, high grading merits being shot on sight without bother of a trial.'

Preacher Tolliver's eyes grew big. Xavier chuckled at the reaction but sobered quickly. 'That would, of course, apply even to an owner who high grades away from partners working on a percentage,' Xavier added as he stared at the professor.

'You know,' Tolliver began in the somewhat pompous voice he used when preaching, 'division of labor is what is called for here. You two do the pick and shovel work and mucking out the cut. I'll separate the good stuff from rock over here. That will be more efficient and faster than each of us doing each job in turn. That's the way a real business would do it.'

'No,' both Xavier and the professor said at the same time.

The professor continued. 'I'll release either of you from the deal now that you've seen how hazardous this situation is.' Preacher Tolliver hesitated for some time but finally shook his head no.

Hayes led them into the cut right up to the wall. Both took a quick intake of breath when they saw the rock up close. Seams of what appeared to be pure gold ran through the exposed surface of the cut down area, inches wide in some areas. Hayes took a small sledge and long chisel, placed it against the edge of one of the seams and hammered the chisel around a chunk the size of several fingers until he opened a seam then took a small pick, inserted it into the crack and prized backwards. After a couple of minutes working the pick, a chunk of gold popped out.

'Take as much as possible of this jewelry stuff as you can; use the big pick or sledge and single jack for bigger chunks. This will go much more slowly, but I think we will get more out before the whole thing comes tumbling down,' the professor told them. 'This will produce several thousand dollars worth, hopefully. Of course, the whole thing might crash down around our ears the first day.'

After they walked back out from underneath the overhang, the professor told them, 'One more thing, and listen carefully to this.' He paused and had their attention. 'I alone will decide when to shut down this operation. No argument. You can walk away any time you wish, but when I say it stops, it stops. I realize that you're operating on a percentage, but you need to know that I'm looking to create a comfortable home for Rachel, to stock this place with pure-blood cattle, and raise quality horse stock. And I want enough of a cushion that I never have to sell my stock when prices are way down. The time is coming when cattle-men who want to survive will have to raise better stock but many fewer than today, especially when the regular rail road comes closer to this area and replaces the little narrow gauge we have now. The narrow gauge is useless for ship-ping livestock. When I feel Rachel and I have enough gold to do what I wish to do with this place, mining stops. I plan to blast this down where no one will ever be tempted to come try to eke out more before it tumbles down. When that time comes, there will be no arguments. You won't have a voice in that decision. Savvy?'

'I might want some of the rock to build on my alfalfa farm,' Xavier said.

Professor Hayes looked quickly at Xavier but said nothing. Try as he might, the professor couldn't visualize the gunfighter as a farmer. He would make it a point to never be on the ladder if Xavier was in a position to bring the cliff down. But he would trust him for a while. He didn't doubt that the Frenchman wanted gold and knew they could get more gold quickly and safely working together. When would the gold be 'enough' for the gunfighter? It was hard enough to figure how to remove gold and not bring the cliff down without trying to watch his backside as well. Could he keep enough focus on his pick work while trying to keep one eye on his partners?

Why did I let these two into this? he asked himself.

CHAPTER SEVENTEEN

Rachel hadn't meant to be gone more than a few minutes until she ran into Hattie Gillis in the millinery shop. She enjoyed Hattie's company more than she had any woman for years despite the difference in their ages. Hattie's enthusiastic acceptance of her invitation to come visit Sunday was ringing in her ears. Her mind raced at what to fix for dinner. She flinched at the boom of thunder and looked at the dark clouds rolling overhead. They'd never get back to the valley before this storm broke. Now she was glad that A.J. had insisted she put his rain slicker into the buckboard before she and Xavier left the valley. Dust blew down the street.

She paid no attention to the woman who stood back in the shadow and watched her walk briskly past the saloon. The sound of a slight scraping in the alley didn't register at all until a callused hand clamped over her mouth and jerked so hard that her feet left the ground. She tried to scream, couldn't, but managed to catch one finger between her teeth and clamped down as hard as she could. A muffled curse was followed by what seemed an explosion inside her head. Pain registered briefly as her shoulders slammed against the wall but disappeared and the world went out of focus. Her teeth released the finger. She felt blood run from her nose into her mouth. 'Hurry up!' one voice urged; a second set of hands clamped on her arms.

Without thinking, she kicked straight upward and heard

a whoosh of breath and a grunt. The hand turned her arms loose but she saw a flash and a hard hand slammed into her face. The slap had the effect of clearing her head briefly. Even so, it took a moment for her to get a breath.

It was more a yell of rage than a scream for help, but another hit to the face cut it short. The hand around her neck turned loose and powerful arms locked around her from the back. She tried to stomp the arch of the man's foot, but missed because she was lifted from the ground. The tall man clamped his hand over her face, carefully keeping his fingers from her teeth. The man behind hustled her toward the back of the saloon; the tall man followed, keeping his hand over her mouth. Rachel tried to resist, but neither her mind nor body seemed to work correctly.

The tall man drew his hand back to hit her again, but suddenly screamed and jumped backwards. Blood flew from his forehead. It took a moment for Rachel to realize that the streak she had seen was a quirt flashing through the air. A bloody welt appeared across the man's nose. He screamed again and grabbed his eye. The quirt whacked twice quickly; the man holding Rachel grunted and released her. Rachel stumbled backwards against the side wall of the saloon. The small woman with the quirt slashed backwards against the tall man.

'You . . .' the shorter man growled and reached toward his gun.

The woman slashed the quirt again, this time across the man's gun hand. 'Threaten me, you pig?' she asked, her voice a growl.

Both men jumped back. 'Where's. . . ?' the shorter asked then stopped.

'He's somewhere near,' the tall one answered. 'He can take care of himself,' he added and ran for the end of the alley where Rachel now saw two horses standing ground hitched.

As the two slashed their horses racing away from the end of the alley, a tall figure ran up, looked toward the two women, pulled his gun and leveled it toward the fleeing men. He hesitated, grasped his left hand underneath his right, lined the pistol on the riders and fired. Both riders leaned lower across their horses at the sound, but otherwise didn't respond. The tall man, who Rachel now recognized as Doc Ramsey, fired again, and squeezed off three more shots without hitting.

Two more men ran past Rachel to the end of the alley. She recognized Xavier, who was to meet her at the wagon in front of the store, and the huge frame of Devlon Gibson. Both drew their pistols, but the riders were now out of pistol range.

The woman tugged on Rachel's arm and drew her through the door and into an office. Rachel looked around in surprise. This wasn't what she had expected when drawn into a door that she presumed went into a storage room for the saloon. A large, roll top, walnut desk was against the wall opposite the alley door. One wall was taken up with cabinets with drawers covering much of the wall. Shelves and shelves of books lined the wall against the alley. Two comfortable-looking stuffed leather chairs sat with a small table between them on which stood a tall kerosene lamp that Rachel recognized immediately as a reading lamp.

'Stops bullets,' the woman told Rachel as she eyed the books.

Despite the chill from the wind and rain as well as the attempted abduction, Rachel laughed. She couldn't tell how she knew, but she knew very well that wasn't the reason for the books. The woman handed Rachel a towel and a heavy woolen shawl. Rachel sopped up as much of the water as possible. The woman was dressed in a dark green, split gabardine riding skirt, a thick white blouse, now wet and plastered against her, and long black boots. A black hat hung from her back, suspended by a chord around her neck. A heavy quirt hung from her right wrist. She had used the quirt with more force than Rachel would have thought such a slight woman could.

'I'm Gaye McWilliams,' the woman told Rachel as she dried herself with another towel.

'I'm Rachel Hayes.'

Gaye laughed. 'I doubt you have to introduce yourself to anyone within a hundred miles.'

'I don't know how to thank you,' Rachel told Gaye.

The door opened. Doc Ramsey, Devlon Gibson, and Xavier trooped in. 'I'm better at patching holes in people than making them,' Doc said.

Gaye looked hard at the three but didn't speak until Xavier stepped from behind Devlon. Gaye's eyes showed surprise but didn't soften. 'Hello, Xavier,' she said.

Rachel turned to her in surprise. 'We've traveled in the same circles, I'm afraid,' Gaye told Rachel.

Xavier tipped his hat slightly to Gaye.

'We don't need any man-help right now,' Gaye told them in a hard voice.

The three looked at each other awkwardly and stepped out. 'I'll be at the wagon,' Xavier told Rachel.

'The two who grabbed you spoke of a third nearby,' Gaye told Rachel.

Rachel remembered as soon as she said it. 'You don't think one of those. . . .' she stopped at the thought.

'I'd bet money on it,' Gaye told her. 'Expect the least from men, and you'll seldom be wrong. Except your professor, of course,' Gaye added with a wry smile.

Rachel smiled slightly in response but stared ahead in concentration.

'Were these two the same ones who attacked you in the teacher house?' Gaye asked after a moment.

Rachel considered a minute, still trying to get her breathing and thinking squared. 'I don't know,' she finally replied. 'One was tall and the other short like the two at our house . . . but everything happened too fast to tell.'

Then Rachel remembered. 'There is one thing,' she told Gaye. 'The smell. I remember the smell from before.'

'What smell?' Gaye asked.

Rachel thought hard but still couldn't identify the smell. 'I'm not sure,' she finally said, frustration in her voice. 'It's something I should recognize but can't.' She considered silently for a long moment then added. 'It just won't come to me. And I can't imagine why a smell sticks out in my mind on both occasions. But if I smell it again, I'll recognize it.'

CHAPTER EIGHTEEN

For the first time since Rachel had become miffed at the professor's curt behavior and apparent jealousy toward Devlon Gibson, she was in a good mood again. Today was to be their first social occasion in their new home. Hattie and Angus Gillis and another family who were homesteading along the edge of the mesa had been invited to come for church and a social. The weather was perfect – almost perfectly clear skies, temperatures mild due to the high elevation of the Hayes valley, mild breeze sweeping down the valley and out of the gap on to the plains. Beneath the large cottonwood that flourished beside the spring and runoff stream, despite the high elevation of the valley, the men had created a platform on which the pump organ rested and several improvised benches created an open air sanctuary-like setting. Adjacent, the table from inside the cabin sat covered in white cloth and beside it another table improvised from boards across stacks of yet unused building stone. Nearby, a bed of hot coals heated a large coffee pot and Dutch ovens from which the odor of browning biscuits wafted.

Preacher Tolliver bustled around the organ and a wooden podium he'd produced from his wagon, managing to stay busy until all the benches and tables had been erected.

Xavier David and Ute transferred dishes from the house to one table while Angus similarly helped Hattie transfer pots from their wagon to the edge of the coals for warming.

'Hattie, you have no idea how good those fresh vegetables smell to me,' Rachel said as she arranged items on the tables. 'Professor, Xavier and Ute, when they're not working the mine or building on the cabin, bunk house, and barn, are helping me turn up a garden for next spring over by the creek where we can irrigate. Seems the men hunger as much for fresh vegetables as I.'

'If you can come over and help me with my canning, I'll share some of this year's crop with you,' Hattie offered. 'I wind up feeding lots of my garden truck to the pigs or chickens 'cause I just don't have time to put it all up,' she said.

'Law, you have no idea how much I'd love to hear hens clucking or pigs grunting,' Rachel said as she worked. 'Of course I know we'll have all that in due time. I never expected to be sleeping in our own cabin and cooking on my own fire this soon.'

'The professor is a real doer,' Hattie told Rachel approvingly. 'Just like my Angus.'

The approach of Professor Hayes and the Brights, who, like Angus and Hattie, had homesteaded land where a spring in a small canyon into the side of the mesa created water flowing for a short distance out on to the plains, cut into their conversation. The Brights were young, two brothers and a sister, and still spoke with a strong brogue from their home in County Down, Ireland. They had been settled longer than the professor and Rachel but a shorter time than Hattie and Angus. 'Notice how Xavier and Preacher Tolliver can't keep their eyes off Bridgette?' Hattie asked behind her hand.

To the side, Professor Hayes, Angus, and the Bright brothers leaned against the Brights' wagon. 'You can have any of the mares you wish for fifty dollars each,' Tom, the oldest brother, told the professor. 'We need to conserve the grazing inside the canyon for the stock we already have and could certainly use the cash.'

'You'll like their stock,' Angus added from the side. 'They've only kept the best. Their mares and your stallion will produce mighty fine stock. Mustang hardiness and thoroughbred speed.'

'I'll take all twenty if they're as good as Angus tells me,' the professor told them.

Patrick, the younger brother and Bridgette smiled happily at each other.

'This will set the youngsters for the next year to get this much cash,' Hattie told Rachel after overhearing the men's conversation. 'They're mighty fine young folk and good neighbors.'

The sound of horses' hoofs drew everyone's attention to the mouth of the canyon. Two riders, tall but not yet identifiable made their way up the valley. Everyone watched silently. Ute faded into the background and Xavier moved into the house.

'Dang!' Professor Hayes finally muttered under his breath and looked even less happy when he saw Rachel smiling broadly at the two.

'Its Devlon and Doc,' she said.

Everyone except the professor visibly relaxed. He frowned even when Angus said, 'I told them about church. Hope you don't mind. I forgot to mention it.'

'Of course not,' Rachel beamed happily. 'I told you and Hattie to tell anyone you saw.'

Everyone except Rachel seemed to notice the lack of enthusiasm on the professor's part. Nevertheless, he stepped forward and offered his hand. 'Get down and come in.'

After shaking hands all around, and holding Rachel's longer than the professor thought necessary, Devlon turned to a large bag hanging from his saddle and removed a beautiful cured ham. 'A little something from the store,' he told them.

Doc Ramsey likewise took something from his saddle-bag, the odor telling everyone that it was freshly baked bread. After handing it to Rachel, he took out a bottle of whiskey and told the men, 'For afterwards.'

'Shall we have church?' Rachel asked as she removed the Dutch ovens and coffee pot further from the hot coals.

The professor welcomed everyone formally and announced that worship would start with music. Hattie stepped to the front. 'We don't have enough books to go around, so we'll stick to hymns that you will probably know,' she said. 'Let's start with *A Mighty Fortress Is Our God.* Everyone familiar?' she asked looking at the Brights. She'd never seen them in Brother Johnnie's church and realized that they might be Catholic, less familiar with the favorite Protestant hymns.

No one commented, so Hattie nodded for Rachel to

play. Hattie nodded to herself with satisfaction when the Brights joined in, obviously knowing the hymn, each with excellent voices. *Guess all the Irish can sing*, Hattie thought as she led the congregation. After that they went through *Rock of Ages, Swing Low Sweet Chariot, Amazing Grace*, and *The Old Rugged Cross*, everyone obviously enjoying the singing. Devlon Gibson had an excellent voice and sang enthusiastically. Hattie smiled to herself when she noticed Ute sitting behind everyone else moving his feet and body rhythmically as if dancing. Doc Ramsey sipped from a cup containing what Hattie presumed to be whiskey, keeping time with his cup and humming rather than singing.

Finally, Professor Hayes stepped forward and announced that it was time for Preacher Tolliver to speak. Before the preacher began, however, Professor Hayes asked Angus to pray. Tolliver was obviously a bit perturbed at someone other than him getting to do the opening prayer, but Rachel nodded quietly at her husband, approving the absence of a long-winded prayer by Tolliver.

Preacher Tolliver began with a very calmly delivered, gentle statement on love and obviously had the group charmed. After a few minutes, though, his presentation became more intense and trickled toward fire and brimstone gaining momentum with every sentence. His face began to turn red; he paused to wipe his forehead with his handkerchief.

As he paused for breath, Professor Hayes stood and faced everyone. 'Thank you, Reverend Tolliver, for those beautiful words. I believe every word you said is something we can carry with us every day. Now Hattie, if you will lead us in one more hymn, I'll ask Angus to dismiss us with prayer. Preacher Tolliver stood with obvious surprise and frustration on his face but quickly recovered his aplomb and joined in enthusiastically when Rachel played and

Hattie began *I Come to the Garden Alone.* Angus quickly followed with a short benediction. Rachel then turned and invited everyone to eat. The women scurried around moving things from inside to the serving table.

Professor Hayes extended his hand to Preacher Tolliver.

'Congratulations, Reverend. That was an excellent sermon. One of the finest and most concise discussions on love that I've ever heard.'

'You didn't let me get started good,' the preacher protested. 'That was just quoting from a preacher at the Baptist Seminary, John Albert Broadus. I didn't even get started on my part.'

'No, you did great!' Professor Hayes enthused. 'Short, sweet, to the point. You knew to end it before you lost anyone. Thank you!' He turned away and Preacher Tolliver stood open-mouthed, uncertain whether Hayes had just praised him or damned him. He recovered, however, and happily accepted the praise everyone gave him individually.

Later, when everyone seemed to have had the last piece of pie they could handle and dawdled over one last cup of coffee, Professor Hayes noticed Ute look toward the entrance to the canyon, quietly ease away, pick up his rifle which had been leaning against one of the piles of unused building stone, and disappear from sight. Without saying anything, the professor also moved away from the group and turned to watch the entrance. A couple of minutes later he heard hoof beats from several horses and noticed five horsemen riding up the canyon toward them. At that distance, he recognized none of the horses or the manner in which any of them rode. From the corner of his eye, he noticed Xavier look down the canyon and quietly ease out of sight. Soon everyone saw the riders. Five men rode abreast. The professor first noticed that all rode exceptionally good horses, well above what cowboys usually had in their string. All wore tied down guns and had rifle stocks visible on the side of their saddles.

'I'll get more coffee cups,' Rachel told the professor although she was obviously nervous about the appearance of this group.

'Try to get the women inside,' the professor told her.

Rachel nodded and called the two women into the house. The professor noticed that the Bright brothers walked to their wagon before walking up beside him. No guns were visible, but Hayes would have bet that each had at least one pistol tucked into their waistbands behind their coats. The five men stopped so that they were spread well apart. No one spoke for a minute. 'Coffee's hot,' the professor finally told them and nodded his head toward the fire.

After a long silence, the rider Hayes had picked as their leader sneered as he spoke. 'Looks like a nesters' convention here.'

Everyone watched the men silently. Finally, the spokesman continued, 'We're from the Double Diamond Cattle Company, and we're losing cattle. I'm the foreman. Pass the word along that we'll not tolerate any squatters on our range, especially not on our water.'

Hayes bristled. 'I purchased a land grant. All the paperwork is filed in Santa Fe.'

'We know that,' the foreman replied, 'and we know the grant stops at the mouth of the canyon. Keep all your stock in the canyon and off our range.'

When no one acknowledged his threat, he continued. 'We're already losing cattle. Everything outside this canyon is our range and our water. You, Irish,' he added looking at the Brights, 'get out and leave the horses. You stole them from our range.'

The Brights moved their coats and uncovered pistols in their waistbands. From the corner of his eye, the professor saw Bridgette step out of the cabin door with a shotgun in her hands. She walked to the corner of the house where any shot she fired, would spray down the line of horsemen.

'They're my horses. I just bought them,' the professor told the gunman.

'You're backing this Irish trash?' the gunman asked. 'This range is for one hundred per cent Americans. Not folks like these.'

'Really?' Professor Hayes asked. 'One hundred per cent Americans? And what are you? Mohawk? Cherokee? Comanche?'

The other gunmen looked puzzled by Hayes' remarks, but the spokesman sneered back, 'This range is for one hundred per cent white Americans, not any kind of heathens; not for red heathens or these mackerel-snapper Irish Catholics.'

'I've filed on one hundred sixty acres outside the canyon entrance,' Xavier said as he stepped around the other corner of the cabin and into sight. 'What about me?'

Two of the gunmen's expressions changed when he appeared. 'Xavier David,' one quietly told the spokesman. 'Texas gunman. Regulator fights. Cattle wars.'

'I mean this range isn't open to Irish dagoes,' the spokesman said, beginning to appear ready to pull in his horns.

'And French?' David asked. He laughed softly. 'Irish Dagoes? Dagoes? You don't even know your bigotry.'

'You Irish got to go,' the gunman repeated. 'You, too, Gillis. I'll ask the boss about the horses, Hayes.'

'And who is your boss?' Hayes asked.

The gunman looked at Gibson and Doc Ramsey, seemed to think a minute before deciding not to answer. The sound of a hammer clicking caught the gunmen's attention. They looked to the side and saw Ute with his rifle across a pile of building stone. He stared back at the gunmen for a moment then put his hand over his mouth. 'Woo woo woo!' he said, patting his mouth, like a dime novel depiction of an Indian warrior. 'I'm a one hundred per cent American native savage; I stake gunmen to ant beds and take scalps.'

The gunmen looked from Ute on one flank to the shotgun on the other and the other armed men facing them and knew they were in no position for gunplay.

'Drag iron if you're going to,' Xavier told him. 'Let's get this on. I'll even turn my back. You're probably more accustomed to shooting people that way.' He turned his back to the gunmen.

The gunmen wanted to save face but also knew they were in no shape for this gunfight. 'No squatters,' the head gunman said and turned away. The others followed quickly.

'Guess they didn't want coffee,' Rachel said with a straight face and broke the long silence as the gunmen rode away.

CHAPTER NINETEEN

Xavier put his foot on the first rung of the ladder but hesitated, staring at the cut into the stone, trying to make himself believe that the part of the rock beyond that already cut away by the professor was not really leaning more than the previous day, but failed to convince himself.

'You sure you want part of this?' Hayes asked Xavier, a bit of a smirk on his face.

The two of them were alone at the site, the preacher instead working on spading up the garden site since there was no build-up of detached rocks to muck up or crush. Besides, the professor wasn't certain he could stand the preacher's company every single day.

After nearly an hour of hammering away with a single

jack and sledge in an awkward position atop the ladder, Xavier stood by the water bucket filled at the spring, wiped his brow and arched backwards, and then twisted side to side as if trying to get his back straight again. 'It's a way to get some cash,' he finally said as if answering a question Hayes hadn't asked.

Hayes shrugged his shoulders and continued to break up rock knocked down by Xavier. 'Aren't you going to ask me why I'm doing this?' he finally asked the professor.

The professor didn't answer for a couple more minutes. 'None of my business,' he finally told Xavier and worked for another couple minutes before he stopped work and joined the gunman at the water bucket. 'I suppose for the same reason as I am.' After drinking a tin dipperful of water, he continued. 'But you've always made your money in a different way.'

'And you?' Xavier questioned. 'You didn't have Rachel as a reason when you started this.'

'I'm sick of using my gun to make money,' the professor told him. 'It ultimately winds up with someone being killed, even though I was always on the side of the law, or at least legal.'

Xavier climbed back up the ladder and started pounded rock again. The professor rolled the cart back to pick up the rock Xavier dropped. 'And it became obvious that being legal didn't always make it right,' the professor added. He returned to work.

'Aren't you going to ask me why I'm claiming land . . . and this insanity?' Xavier asked waving his hand toward the rock hanging over both of them. 'And this is insanity, you know,' he told Hayes.

'You're like the cork in the neck of the bottle; you can block this valley,' Hayes told him.

Xavier laughed in a humorless manner. 'You should

know I check things as carefully as you do. That's probably why we're both alive after the way we've lived.'

The professor stopped and looked questioningly at Xavier.

'I know about the ingress and egress rights to this valley guaranteed in your title. I know you're not blocked by my land. It took me a while before I discovered that. I figured there had to be some reason you didn't claim the land yourself to keep from being blocked.'

'OK, I'll play. Why did you claim the land?' the professor asked.

'Look, Captain . . . I mean Professor. One reason both of us are probably alive is that we avoided a shootout where it was one of us versus the other. I figured you're almost good as I am, and neither of us would make it out unmarked, likely neither of us alive or, at least so shot to hell life wouldn't be worth living.' He paused. The professor waited for him to continue. 'How many times have you been shot, Professor?'

The professor was surprised and quiet for a long moment. 'Four,' he finally answered. 'Fortunately none too major.'

'Three here,' Xavier answered, 'two of them bad. I don't want any more of it, especially for someone else to pay me a few dollars to do the bleeding while they make a pile of money. I figure I might be lucky enough to live through one more battle or war, but it can't last forever.'

The professor casually shifted his weight toward his Henry leaning against the rock wall. Xavier laughed, this time genuinely mirthful. 'Not with you, Professor; not with you.'

'Then why?' Hayes asked.

'I want to raise cows, fine cows. In France . . . in Ariège Province, the Pyrenees Mountains, my family had some cows, some sheep, a few goats, and horses. Big horses, Professor, descended from the war horses of the knights. Enough maize – corn – for the livestock. My family made cheese from milk of ewes.' He chuckled at the professor's surprise at that. 'In France, Professor, we make cheese from every kind of milk: cows, goats, sheep, mares. . . .'

Xavier returned to his work with single jack and sledge for several minutes. 'But it is beef cattle I want to raise, Professor, big, white cattle from Burgandy – cross them with American Herefords and some longhorns. Ah, Professor. You could make some fine cattle, long enough legs to walk to market, very large bodies, but hardy enough for this climate. Alfalfa and corn, range grass and water. . . . Buy my horses from you, of course, Professor.'

Hayes didn't talk again, but he thought long and deeply about whether or not to believe Xavier. He certainly sounded sincere, and it did mirror his own thoughts and motives, but . . . *dammit!* That was the problem with his gun-fighting career. Who to believe and to trust? And Xavier did show up shortly after Rachel was beaten up by the gunmen hunting his gold.

CHAPTER TWENTY

The following morning, the professor and Xavier were in the saddle before sunrise on their way to the Brights' homestead. By mid-morning, they pulled up in front of the wide opening into an even larger valley that, like the professor and Rachel's valley, sloped upward to the top of the flat mesa. Near the back end of the gap, where it widened into a big valley, three cabins stood within one hundred feet of each other, a larger stone cabin in the center flanked by two log cabins that the professor would estimate as no more than the sixteen feet square that met the requirements of taking up public domain under the Homestead Act of 1862. Several large trees shaded much of the area around the cabins.

Also visible were a large barn with stone walls to the height of about twelve feet and then timber walls for about another twelve feet. Double doors stood open and revealed stalls down one side, stacked hay on the other. An opening on the second floor revealed another set of doors to a second floor. Several corrals were scattered as well as two other buildings, smaller than the big barn. One was a sod cabin approximately sixteen feet square. Rail fences, uncommon in New Mexico, surrounded what appeared to be a large vegetable growing plot. To the professor's right, a rail fence cut off the opening to a side valley, plowed ground with spikes of green showing. What appeared to be about thirty horses occupied the two largest corrals. Other horses, a few cows, and a few sheep were scattered through the valley.

'They've done a heck of a lot of work for supposed thieves,' Xavier commented. 'I never knew many thieves that favored hard labor.'

'From the looks of these buildings, they could make a right good living as builders,' the professor said. 'Angus told me that the three cabins are each in the corner of a quarter section homesteaded by each of the Brights. They've claimed four hundred and eighty acres and are waiting to hire hands to file claims on a couple more quarter sections. And they control access to the timberlands beyond them.'

'A beautiful setup,' Xavier commented.

'And a beautiful single lady, X,' the professor added.

Xavier looked surprised as he turned to the professor. 'Be damn, Professor! Yesterday you were ready to shoot me and today you're trying to marry me off to the neighbor woman.' He didn't miss the use of the nickname, 'X,' nicknames being a habitual way in which the professor referred to friends.

'If you married her, you'd probably move over here,

wouldn't you?' the professor asked, and gigged his horse into motion before Xavier could read his expression or body language.

Bridgette and Tom came out of the bigger house to meet them, and a rider came from the ridge overlooking the gap toward the house, arriving at almost the same time as the visitors. 'Good morning, Professor,' Bridgette said, and turned toward Xavier, who received an even brighter smile than he, the professor noticed. '*Bonjour*, Xavier. *Comment allez-vous?*' she said.

Xavier's face registered his surprise at her use of French. '*Très bien*, Bridgette,' he responded and bowed slightly, his hat in his hand. '*Et vous?*' he asked.

'*Très bien, aussi*,' she responded, her face slightly flushed.

'I so seldom hear French,' Xavier commented. 'It is such a treat.'

'That just about exhausts my conversational French,' Bridgette responded, smiling. 'But I'm willing to learn more,' she added and blushed noticeably.

Tom greeted both and looked at the professor, his surprise at the exchange evident. Patrick dismounted and greeted the guests. The professor was struck again at how much the brothers resembled – could almost pass for twins, he thought – except that Patrick had soot-black hair while Tom's was deep red, like Bridgette's. All three had very bright blue eyes. Bridgette was tall, probably as tall as Rachel, the professor judged, and truly, strikingly pretty as he had told Xavier. He had been teasing Xavier about the pretty girl, but saw obvious attraction between the two.

'Please, come in for some coffee,' Bridgette said and turned toward the porch.

Patrick took the reins of Xavier's and the professor's horses as well as his own and led them toward the barn. 'I'll take care of these,' he told them.

A wide porch cast a deep shadow against the house. Inside, one entered a large room with a cast-iron stove, built-in cabinets, and a table with six chairs on one side of the room, as well as a fireplace and several chairs, including rockers, on the opposite side. A thick slab of what appeared to the professor to be cedar made a mantle. At least two dozen books sat on it. Doors led to two other rooms in the back. The professor could see a bright patchwork quilt covering a bed in one room. Each of the three walls he could see had a small window with shutters of thick lumber on each. In addition, there were several of what appeared to be windows except for being covered over by heavy timber with gun loops through them.

'We hope to open up windows in those spots, someday,' Tom told the professor as he handed him a cup of coffee. 'Unfortunately, right now we have to think of defense.'

'As in the castles in your home country,' the professor nodded.

'There have been shots several times,' Bridgette told them as she set a pie with plates on the table. 'Please join us.'

'Nothing brings thoughts of home so much as the smell of coffee and baking,' Xavier said as he took Bridgette's chair and seated her.

This domesticity just didn't square with his ideas of the Frenchman, the professor thought. Could he possibly be sincere about a home and farm, perhaps hanging the guns on the wall? After all, no one could have been more surprised when former gunman and Texas Ranger A.J. Hayes stepped out on to the train platform and asked Rachel McNew to marry him.

The professor couldn't remember the last time he had dawdled for an entire hour over coffee before marrying Rachel and now visiting his neighbors. The four men plus Bridgette leaned against the railing of the corral with twenty mares within it. They had done the pro forma haggling about price, but the professor knew from the start that he wanted these twenty mares. They were mustangs captured by the Brights and now seemed remarkably tamed rather than broken. None were more than five years old, were sound, well framed and muscled, and had obviously been on good grub in this valley.

'Well hell's bells, Professor! I have bread in the oven inside. Are you going to buy these or not?' Bridgette blurted out.

The professor didn't pause in cleaning his nails with the point of his pocket knife, nor did he look up for what seemed a long moment.

Finally, he burst out laughing. 'Why yes, Miss Bright, I believe I will take all twenty,' and thrust out his hand to shake with her. 'In fact, I have the money in my saddle-bags.' He laughed again and shook hands with both of the brothers, and walked toward the barn, Tom by his side.

'I don't think you need my help with this part,' Xavier told the professor. 'I'll help Bridgette, instead.'

The professor didn't speak but waved his hand over his shoulder as he walked away to signal his agreement. 'I don't have many cattle right now, Tom, but I see you have two bulls out there that look like Red Devon. Keep in mind, before you sell one, that I will be interested at some point.'

A gunshot ripped the air and a bullet sang right by the professor's ear, ricocheting loudly off the stone wall of the barn. Tom pushed the professor the last few steps into the barn, yanked him to the side and looked him over quickly. 'I thought you were hit,' Tom said.

The professor popped back up. 'Bridgette. . . .' he started.

'Inside the house with Xavier,' Tom said, and at the same time grabbed a rifle from where it stood by the door.

The professor jumped behind the stone portion of the barn's wall and peered out. Riders raced toward them, probably a dozen at least, he figured. He laid his pistol barrel on one of the heavy timbers of the barn gate, sighted on the nearest rider and squeezed. The rider jerked hard and dropped his pistol, grabbed the saddle-horn, but steadied himself and rode on by.

The professor looked toward the main house and saw the shutters closed over the windows. Just as he watched, smoke exploded from the ports on two windows. A horse plunged, rolled, and struggled to get back to his feet but failed. The rider lay stunned for a moment before he got up and ran toward the wall of one of the cabins. A puff of smoke came from the loophole in the shutters of that cabin.

'I have the back!' Tom yelled and raced for the back door of the barn. Another puff of gunsmoke came from the small soddy. Something bothered the professor about that, but he didn't have time to think about it as the raiders swept back through the yard. He heard Tom fire from the back door. Two of the attackers swept around the corner of the barn toward the professor, not more than twenty feet away. Both fired rapidly with their revolvers. Chips of stone and wood flew around the professor as their bullets struck nearby.

He dropped to the ground to escape the spattered missiles. He fired twice quickly at the nearest rider, striking him twice in the chest. He flew backwards from his horse. The other rider wheeled his horse and lay against the horse, Indian style. Hayes fired twice at him but missed.

He raced to the first stall where he saw his horse twisting around, nervous from all the shooting, reached over the stall wall and grabbed his Henry rifle from its saddle scabbard. A quick glance showed Tom hunkered by the wall looking for a target. The professor ran back to his spot, just in time to snap a shot at another rider racing by.

The deep boom of a shotgun caught his attention; a rider near the house flew backwards out of his saddle. From the other window a pistol fired and another rider fell from his horse. The raiders had had enough.

Obviously having run into more than they expected, they raced away. The professor aimed at one, elevated his sights and squeezed off one last shot. The rider jerked, grabbed his right arm, but managed to hang in the saddle. The sudden quiet was almost as startling as the noise had been.

'Clear on that side?' Tom called out.

'Clear,' the professor answered as he stepped outside and looked quickly from side to side to confirm it.

Patrick emerged from the nearest cabin just before Xavier and Bridgette did so from the house. All four appeared to be uninjured, the professor noted with satisfaction. Bridgette still carried her shotgun. She looked at the man shot down with the shotgun and turned away, not completely at ease with having just shot a man, but also not breaking down, the professor noted.

'Professor,' Xavier said, and motioned him over to the horse lying dead now in the yard. 'The brand.'

The professor looked and nodded. 'Why am I not surprised?' he asked.

'These also,' Patrick said, leading two of the raiders' mounts to them.

'Double diamond,' Bridgette said to herself.

CHAPTER TWENTY-ONE

'Fastest I ever saw a reward work,' Devlon told the sheriff.

Sheriff Swede Kittelson, Devlon Gibson, Pitts Randall,

and the man the professor remembered as the foreman of the Double Diamond stood in front of the sheriff's office. Curious townspeople began to drift down at the sight of three dead men across the backs of the two horses with the Double Diamond brand.

The professor was rather taken by Devlon's remark. 'Reward?' he asked.

'Those the men?' Sheriff Kittelson asked the foreman. 'Jack McGinness, here, foreman of the Double Diamond,' Kittelson indicated the big white-haired man, 'just posted a reward for these men for stealing Double Diamond horses. And the horses?' he added.

The foreman stepped to the bodies, raised their heads to where he could see their faces, and nodded. 'This is them.'

'These and several others attacked our place,' Tom told the sheriff.

'These three are renegades,' the foreman said. 'Probably a falling out among thieves, these and those Irishers,' he said, pointing toward Tom. 'Bunch of nester trash, all of them.'

Tom turned his horse to face the foreman. 'You calling me a thief? You're wearing a gun,' he said.

The foreman's hand crept toward his pistol.

'Enough!' the sheriff snapped and stepped between the two, holding one hand up toward each. He let his hand drop by his own pistol. 'I'll take down the first one of you that moves toward your gun!'

The professor didn't know the sheriff well, but he struck him as someone who could back up what he said. 'Not now, Tom,' the professor said. Out of the corner of his eye, he saw Xavier turn his horse so that he faced Pitts Randall. He kept his own eyes on Devlon Gibson, who had a pistol stuck inside his waist. He knew that he didn't have to say anything to Xavier; he'd been in shooting situations before.

During the time he and Rachel had lived in town, the

professor had had several conversations with the sheriff and considered him a very solid man and suspected he would be quite salty if forced into gunplay. Those spectators nearest the participants tried to ease back away from possible shots but found others behind them unwilling to move.

'I have a court hearing in a few minutes,' Sheriff Kittelson said, 'but tomorrow morning I'll be at the Brights' no later than eight o'clock. Don't move or change anything. I'll want to see bloodstains, bullet scars, the dead horse. Sorry to ask a lady like your sister to put up with that,' he told Tom.

The foreman appeared about to say something when the sheriff referred to Bridgette as a lady, but the sheriff's face dissuaded him. The professor looked toward Devlon and Pitts. 'Gentlemen, please feel free to join us at the Bright ranch tomorrow morning if you have questions.'

Pitts and Devlon exchanged a quick look and began to walk down the sidewalk toward Devlon's office.

'During all the shooting, the mares I had come to pick up broke down the corral fence and scattered. We'll have to gather and drive them back to my place tomorrow, anyway,' the professor said.

'That's stolen stock! Rounded up on our range,' the foreman told the sheriff angrily.

Tom had begun turning his horse away but swung it back toward the foreman and eased his hand toward his pistol again. The sheriff stepped between Tom and the foreman again. 'I'll check the brands tomorrow, naturally,' he told him. 'Please bring any paperwork to support your charges. Remember that unbranded mustangs traditionally belong to whoever captures them. By the way,' he added, 'who owns the Double Diamond?'

The sheriff watched the foreman with obvious interest. Devlon and Pitts had started down the sidewalk toward

Devlon's office, but stopped and turned, their eyes intently staring at the foreman. The foreman cast his eyes toward Devlon and Pitts but quickly back toward the sheriff. 'Scottish investors,' the foreman answered. He turned away angrily and reached to take the lead lines of the horses bearing the dead men.

'I'm impounding the horses and bodies until completion of my investigation,' the sheriff said.

The foreman mounted, yanked his horse around and spurred it viciously in the sides. Two other riders the professor hadn't noticed before followed the foreman away, on their Double Diamond branded horses, he saw.

'I'll also withhold the reward money until conclusion of the investigation,' the sheriff told the professor.

A few minutes later, the professor, Xavier, and Tom sat with Gaye McWilliams at a table in her saloon. 'What do you know about the Double Diamond ranch and management?' the professor asked Gaye.

She looked surprised, seemed to consider something for a long moment, then finally shrugged and answered, 'I was surprised to hear the foreman say Scottish investors. Pitt Randall owns a share in the Double Diamond.' She sipped on her brandy seemingly trying to decide how much to reveal. 'Who knows,' she finally said. 'Devlon and Pitt share in several businesses, although few here know that. And don't repeat that I said it,' she said emphatically. 'I've done well here by keeping my mouth shut and my nose out of other people's business.'

Xavier turned to the professor. 'You suppose some of your ranger friends would know anything about these people?'

'Devlon's not lily-white,' Gaye told them. 'I'm pretty sure he owns a share in Pitt's bordello. . . .' She hesitated for a moment, finally took another sip, and shook her head. 'But I don't think he's a thief or killer. Wouldn't be his way.' After a moment, she added, 'They didn't seem to know about the gold at your place until you showed up on the fourth of July.'

All of them drank their liquor silently for several minutes. 'I heard you tell the sheriff that you will meet him at the Brights' tomorrow morning,' Gaye finally told the professor. 'As angry as the Double Diamond foreman looks, I think I'd bring Rachel here rather than leave her alone at your ranch.'

'The preacher would be there with her,' the professor answered doubtfully.

'Like I said, don't leave her alone,' Gaye reiterated.

'We could use another hand,' the professor told Gaye. 'Someone to work and who would stand in case of gunplay.'

'Mose McGuire,' Gaye said. 'Good blacksmith, stonecutter, and mason and can shoot the eye out of a gnat with his old Walker Colt or shotgun. Maybe the best fiddler I ever heard. I'll have him here in the morning when you bring Rachel.'

CHAPTER TWENTY-TWO

'*Mon dieu*! That's the ugliest son ... homeliest beast I've ever seen!' Xavier said as they stopped their horses in their tracks. Outside the entrance to Gaye McWilliams' private quarters, a huge brindle mule turned an eye on them and bared its teeth like a dog growling, his ears flat back against his head, his head twisted to the side and seemingly set to charge, which was more of a concern than usual because the mule wasn't hitched or tied. They could see nothing to stop the animal coming after them. The wagon to which he was hitched was large, its sideboards made out of what appeared to be heavy two-by-twelves, at least four feet high with canvas snugged down tight over the top.

Xavier nodded his head toward a Colt's revolving shotgun leaning against the side of the wagon to bring the professor's attention to it, as all three dismounted. Both noticed a large dog underneath the wagon watching them silently. The dog was perhaps the biggest he had ever seen, the professor thought, and certainly the most daunting. Surely, he figured, it must weigh well over one hundred pounds; fangs stuck out of the lips, looking like the cutting apparatus of a razorback hog. The dog's face looked like it had been cut up and sewed back together without all the pieces in the right places. Both ears were ragged, but the left looked like it had been shredded. 'Don't know which I'd worry about more if I wanted to mess with the wagon: the dog or the mule,' the professor told Xavier. 'If one don't get you, the other'n will!' he added in sing-song.

'Lawd a mercy! You gentlemens don't get too close to Sweet Pea! She bites worser 'n any grizzly bear you ever seen.'

Xavier and the professor had been so intent on the wagons and animals that they hadn't noticed the door opening. They gawked at the hulk filling the door. He must be at least six and one half feet tall, the professor figured, and perhaps two axe handles wide from the shoulders, pretty much on down all the way to the ground, ending in the largest boots the professor had ever seen. His skin was coal black except for a light-colored scar across his left cheek. His head was shaved as slick as a peeled onion; he held a black felt hat in his left hand. It was several moments before the professor noticed Gaye McWilliams standing beside the behemoth, the tip of her head not coming anywhere near his armpits.

Rachel was the first to break off her stare and step to Gaye and embrace her in a hug. Even Rachel, who was several inches taller than the professor, didn't reach to the man's shoulders. The professor and Xavier could still do nothing but stare; neither had ever seen a human nearly this large. The giant smiled patiently at them as they gawked. 'This is Mose McGuire,' Gaye finally told them.

The pressure of Rachel's foot against his leg, made the professor break out of the apparent trance. 'A.J. Hayes,' the professor managed as he offered his hand. Manners or no manners, the professor couldn't help but stare toward their hand clasp. McGuire's hand engulfed the professor's as the professor's might engulf a newborn infant. The fingers and palm of McGuire's hands were hard and calloused enough to strike matches on them, but the impression was more a tender and gentle strength.

'And Xavier David,' the professor said as he nodded toward Xavier. Xavier's expression and look toward McGuire's hands indicated that his reaction to the hand was the same.

'You need Mose,' Gaye told the professor. 'He is the best blacksmith, stone mason, and builder I've ever seen. If he can't do it, it doesn't really need to be done. And,' she added, 'he will be excellent security for your ranch and for Rachel.'

'And this, Mose,' Gaye said, 'is Rachel Hayes, the lady I told you about.'

Mose nodded several times and semi-bowed before he took Rachel's proffered hand. 'Yes'm, Mrs Hayes, a pleasure,' he said.

The professor watched Rachel's face to see her reaction to the huge, rough-skinned hand. Unlike the professor and Xavier, Rachel appeared to see nothing unusual about his hand. 'It is my pleasure, Mr McGuire,' she told him. The smile on her face told the professor all he needed to accept the big man.

'We welcome you, Mose,' he said. 'Our efforts at cabin building could definitely use a skilled touch. And we hope to be putting a blacksmith to work as well as we build a horse herd. Will fifty and found do to start with?' he asked.

'Yassuh, that be fine,' Mose said and bowed his head again.

The professor couldn't say why, but he felt that the accent and obsequious manner wasn't the real Mose, but he knew many black people had learned to play the role in the South. Mose did, however, make direct eye contact, the professor thought, pleased. With all the trouble that seemed to be brewing, he wanted someone to be aggressive in protecting Rachel; he wasn't sure why, but he felt Gaye wouldn't recommend Mose unless he was well qualified. *Qualified, hell*, the professor decided. *This man could go bear-hunting with a switch, and he had a hunch Mose also knew how to use the Colt revolving shotgun in his wagon.*

'That be Tarbaby,' Mose said and pointed to the dog underneath the wagon. 'Come here, Tarbaby,' he said. The dog rose and walked toward his owner but obviously kept everyone within sight. Mose took Rachel's hand and held it toward the dog. 'Tarbaby, this is Mrs Hayes. She's good.' Tarbaby sniffed the hand and wagged his stubby tail. Mose did the same with the other two. 'OK, Tarbaby,' Mose said. The dog returned to its place underneath the wagon.

'Tarbaby has to be at least half bear,' Xavier commented, unable to take his eyes off the dog.

'Yessir,' Mose replied, 'Tarbaby's half bear, half dog, half horse and half alligator with just a tetch of snapping turtle.'

The professor chuckled, but somehow didn't doubt any part of the stated pedigree.

'Mr McGuire,' the professor began.

'It's just plain Mose,' McGuire interrupted. 'I won't know who you're talking to iffen you call me Mister.'

'OK, Mose,' the professor said, and handed Mose several gold coins. 'If you have room in your wagon, go buy the materials you need to set up your smithy shop as well as to

115

build. We'll be needing horse shoes, hinges, branding irons, and whatever you will need to build a house. If you have change left, count it as advance on your first month's pay.'

'And won't you all come in?' Gaye asked and stepped aside.

CHAPTER TWENTY-THREE

'Tea and scones! I can't believe it!' Rachel said. 'My mother grew up in England. She made scones so much like these. Unfortunately, I never learned from her.'

'You will be able to have scones anytime you wish, now,' Gaye told her with a mysterious smile on her face.

Rachel waited expectantly for Gaye to tell her how or why she could now have scones whenever she wished. 'I can't ride in here that often,' Rachel finally said.

Gaye simply smiled again and shook her head no. Finally, she spoke. 'Mose made these,' she said. 'Now I'll be wishing for scones just out of the oven, and you will have them whenever you wish. I might show up on your doorstep begging.'

Rachel was stunned. She couldn't imagine the hulking giant cooking something as delicate as scones. 'And you won't believe what he can do with wild game and beef from these old range cows around here,' Gaye told her.

'A.J. and I might have to wrestle to see who gets his services more hours,' Rachel said chuckling.

They drank their tea and ate their scones silently for a while. Finally, Rachel sat her tea cup down and leaned forward. 'You seem to know more about what is going on around here than anyone else, Gaye. A.J. tells me everything he knows. He believes that no one here knew about the gold in our valley until the Fourth of July race, but he tells me that he saw Double Diamond riders exploring our basin before anyone knew about his buying it. And why are they so determined to drive out the Brights but have never bothered the Gillises?'

'Have you or the professor heard the railroad rumors?' Gaye asked as she poured more tea.

Rachel was shocked; she sat silently thinking. Gaye waited patiently for Rachel to process the information and its ramifications. Gaye was silently tickled to discover the small dimples that appeared in Rachel's cheeks when she was so deep in thought. The professor had done himself proud when he stepped out at the RR depot and sought Rachel's hand, despite Pitt's scary presence. She felt fond warmth when she remembered Rachel's defiance of the big man and also when she remembered how small and unimposing the professor looked against Pitt. *Damned if I don't wish I had gone East and caught on that marriage train myself.* But on the other hand, she found herself feeling a sister's or even mother's affection and concern for Rachel. *Certainly she is young enough to be my daughter,* Gaye thought.

'I've heard nothing,' Rachel said. 'And I'm sure the professor would have told me if he knows. But I came in on the railroad. What do you mean?'

'The current line is a very lightweight, narrow gauge route. I bless it because it keeps this town alive, but it is extremely limited in what it can carry in way of freight and people. You remember how uncomfortable it was. They propose to bring a much heavier, standard gauge railroad down through Raton Pass to Santa Fe and onward, perhaps to Mexico City, perhaps west to California or even both. It could make a very profitable line: the army, especially with the Indians acting up; the reservations like Ft Sumner and ones that will be set up for Apaches; and I believe that there is going to be a tremendous mining boom, not only gold and silver but other metals like copper and lead and manganese. All could create tremendous freight business, not even counting passengers.'

Gaye allowed Rachel several minutes to digest this information. Finally, she spoke again. 'Some things people seldom think about with railroad construction, for example, cross-ties. Railroads will pay a premium for cross-ties cut nearby to save shipping expense. The only access to the local highlands with timber suitable for cross-ties goes through your ranch or the Brights'. The Brights have even more access to highland timber than you do, but your timber would make quite a bit of money, also.'

'And no one can cut the timber without coming through the Brights and us,' Rachel said to herself.

'Nor without going through Xavier's land,' Gaye pointed out.

Rachel's eyes got bigger.

'How much do you know about Xavier, Rachel?' Gaye asked quietly.

CHAPTER TWENTY-FOUR

The professor and Xavier met Sheriff Kittelson as they left town. The sheriff rode a big black mule larger than most western saddle horses, a mule with a gait nearly as soft as the professor's Napoleon. The professor chuckled to himself at the sight of the sheriff. He had already noticed that he wore his pants so low that much of his butt was above his belt, but was nevertheless surprised to see his belt riding all the way below his butt on the saddle. *Looks like it would chafe his cheeks*, the professor thought. The long gun in his saddle scabbard appeared to be a shotgun; an old Walker Colt revolver of Mexican War vintage also rode on his saddle, almost certainly converted from cap and ball, to metal cartridges, he figured. His gun-belt, which unlike the belt in his britches, rode above his waist, held a .36 caliber Navy Colt, definitely converted to cartridges, because the loops were all filled with .36 caliber cartridges. Talk the professor had heard around town indicated that Kittelson was reasonably quick with the pistol and uncannily accurate, as well as totally unflappable in the face of danger.

'You have a really nice crop this year,' the professor told him as they passed by several acres of corn, beans, peppers, and vegetables, surrounded by a rail fence.

'Yah, if I can keep the deer out of it,' he said. 'My lazy dogs want to sleep on my porch rather than in the field. I am trying to stop the deer during this full moon. I've killed four this week at night. Killing them faster than my wife can smoke them. Hopefully they'll quit coming into my field.'

The professor pulled his horse up to a quick halt and sat staring at a large tower under construction not far from the sheriff's corn field. 'What . . . is that?' he finally asked, pointing to the huge structure in progress. 'This is part of another experiment,' the sheriff answered proudly. 'From the top, there will be an uninterrupted line of sight to each of the nearest mountains or buttes as well as town and the army post.'

The professor and Xavier sat silently for what seemed a long time. 'For what purpose?' Xavier finally asked.

'A new communication system,' the sheriff answered proudly. 'It will probably be years before telegraph lines connect towns in this area, but the sun shines almost every day.'

'Smoke signals?' Xavier finally asked.

'Mirrors,' the sheriff responded proudly. 'Only one person on each tower and mirrors could flash reflections of sunlight from one signal tower to the next. Then the person at the receiving tower could relay to those nearest and on down the line. It could travel almost as fast as a telegraph without having to use all those posts and wire.'

'In the daytime,' Xavier finally responded.

'Yah, but at night one could have a firebox with reflectors. It could work just as well. Perhaps you would even put one of these on your highest point, Professor. The Brights and the Gillises, too. You could all have communication without the travel. Perhaps have an agreed upon time to mount your tower to check for messages; perhaps just after the midday meal or right after sunrise.'

'Very interesting,' the professor said. He realized that he didn't sound sincere, but he actually did mean it was interesting. 'It certainly makes sense for the army, especially, to the deserts to the South as well as in West Texas.'

For several minutes, they rode silently, the sheriff seemingly deep in thought. 'Those Brights,' Kittelson finally said and then paused. 'They seem to be good young people. The Double Diamond ought to be grateful that they catch mustangs. Those mustangs eat grass and drink water that the ranch would seem to want for their cows.'

'The Brights work harder than I've seen any thieves work,' Xavier said.

The sheriff cut his eyes toward Xavier but said nothing, as if he was evaluating the Frenchman. It reminded the professor that Xavier's reputation among lawmen wasn't considered too lily-white. He let his mind run back over his own doubts about Xavier and over everything that had happened since he had come into this country. He couldn't see any reason to fault the gunman; he'd worked hard for the professor and Rachel as well as fought well against the Double Diamond raiders at the Brights' ranch, in fact apparently killed one of the raiders and winged another. *Why is he up here in this area*, the professor wondered again? *Had he perhaps been involved in the recent shooting difficulties down in Lincoln County?*

'The reward will add up to seven hundred fifty dollars, if everything checks out,' Kittelson said. 'I have the bank holding the money. McGinness had just come in and posted the reward before you arrived yesterday with the dead men. Said that the three men had stolen Double Diamond horses and left.'

'Only three?' Xavier asked? 'There were more raiders than that.'

'Yah. Rather peculiar that you killed three out of the group, and they exactly matched the ones McGinness listed,' Kittelson mused. After a couple of minutes, Kittelson asked, 'Did you notice how lathered McGinness's horse was? It had been ridden very hard.'

Around mid-morning, the professor, Xavier, and Sheriff Kittelson rode into the Brights' valley. Tom was sitting on the front porch braiding a rawhide riata; Patrick was working a saddle horse on reining in the smaller of the corrals. The horses the professor had bought were in the largest corral again. Bridgette stepped on to the porch, wiping her hands on her apron as the three rode up. Her smile was pleasant, the professor noticed, but especially brightened when she looked at Xavier. *I hope Xavier is on the level with this domestic bent he's showing*, the professor thought. *If he hurts this girl. . . .* He had to chuckle at himself as he

121

realized that he sounded like an old patriarch of a family. Tom Bright's steely blue eyes reminded the professor that it wouldn't be up to him to punish the transgressions of any man against Bridgette.

Sheriff Kittelson looked around, taking in the solid barn, cabins, the green crop protected by a rail fence, the fine horses in the large corral, and Patrick working the mustang in such a gentle manner. 'How do you keep deer and elk from eating your crop?' he asked, nodding to the field.

'Dogs,' Tom answered. 'When I can keep Bridgette from petting them, they roam the fields and around the barns at night.'

Kittelson nodded approvingly. 'My dogs. . . .' He shook his head in disgust. He started, quickly looking down at his feet to find a large black mama cat, which obviously would soon have kittens. 'Ah,' he said, kneeling to pet the cat. 'I'd almost rather have one of your cats than one of your fine bulls. So close to town I am, mice and rats are a bother.'

'Patrick's in charge of horses, I of cows; Bridgette is the cat wrangler,' Tom said smiling.

'It just so happens,' Bridgette said as she kneeled and picked up the cat, 'that I think I'm going to be looking for a home for a few kittens pretty soon.' She stood and handed the cat to the sheriff. He took the cat, which rubbed her head against him. 'See?' Bridgette said, 'she is already marking you as her territory.'

The sheriff's face darkened as he looked toward the entry to the valley where five riders approached. 'Would you take my cat and stay inside?' he asked and handed the cat back to Bridgette.

Xavier drifted down to one end of the porch and the professor eased further away in the opposite direction. As he did so, he noticed Patrick move into the opening of the barn. Did he just see the door of the soddy in the yard open very slightly? he wondered.

His eyes were attracted to the thick shutters closing over the windows in the house. He smiled inwardly when he saw a couple of inches of the tip of a double-barreled shotgun emerge from the shooting loop in one of the windows. Tom moved a few feet to his left, taking himself further from that window and shotgun. As the riders pulled up in front of the Brights' cabin and stopped with five or more feet between each, he noticed the two riders nearest the window look at the shotgun and then at each other. The shotgun barrel moved the slightest bit, tracking the rider on the end as he edged his horse to the side.

The Double Diamond riders' mounts were all better than the cow ponies on most cow outfits, the professor noticed again, as he had done when the Double Diamond riders had visited his own valley. They were taller, longer-legged than the more compact cutting horses most ranches furnished, most from mustang stock. These riders' horses would certainly outdistance most ranch horses in a chase, but wouldn't be as agile working stock and subsisting primarily on grass rather than grain, as most ranch horses did, wouldn't serve these horses well. All the men wore their guns as if they were part of them; whenever most cowhands wore a gun, the professor thought, the guns looked out of place on them.

Near the other end of the porch, the professor noticed Xavier loosen his gun in his holster and hook his thumbs in his belt, his right hand close to his holstered pistol; with his left hand, he brushed the second gun stuck in his belt behind his back, as if reassuring himself it was in place. Actually, the professor knew that Xavier hadn't needed to reassure himself where the second gun was located, but rather wanted the Double Diamond riders to think about the fact that he would have twelve shots, provided that both were full of cartridges and that two guns would be blazing in any shootout that might take place. The professor had done the same thing when he was a ranger, messing with the minds of potential adversaries.

Sheriff Kittelson hitched his pants up over his butt and in the process wound up with his hand close to his Navy Colt, the professor noticed. The Swede had been in a shooting rodeo or three, himself, he could tell. The professor was amused despite the tense situation. And the situation was tense! The Double Diamond riders might just as well have been wearing war-paint, their hostility was so evident.

'Gentlemen,' Kittelson began, his accent much thicker than usual, 'perhaps Miss Bright has some coffee on the fire.'

'We're not here for coffee,' McGinnness responded coldly.

'Ah, so let us look at the evidence, then,' Kittelson said, and walked toward the corner of the house. 'Mr McGinness, leave your riders here,' he said, 'and Professor Hayes and Mr David, please wait here as well. 'And,' he added with a nod toward the shotgun, 'Miss Bright as well.'

The two riders who hadn't noticed Bridgette's shotgun followed the Swede's eyes; it was crystal clear that they all saw the shotgun, now. The professor could almost see their horns pulling back. The rider on the end nearest Bridgette's shotgun started to sidle his horse slowly to the side. The tip of Bridgette's shotgun turned to track the rider.

'I believe the sheriff asked us all to stay where we are,' Xavier said quietly.

The professor clearly heard the click of hammers being cocked behind Bridgette's window. The riders stiffened visibly. Xavier smiled appreciatively. 'Let's all sit quietly, men,' he said. 'And Bridgette, should any trouble break out, you take the two middle riders with that ten-gauge. I'll take this one,' he said quietly, 'and Ranger Hayes, you the one on the end. But I really bet I can get both of these two before they clear leather.'

The professor didn't like these men, but was glad they were professional gunmen. They would know their odds of shooting from a horse versus three on the ground, two of them proficient gunfighters and the other with a shotgun. Amateurs might have bucked those odds; money fighters wouldn't.

'Which one you want me to take?' Patrick called from the barn.

The Double Diamond riders cut their eyes toward the barn and saw the muzzle of a Spencer carbine resting on the gate.

'Just shoot whichever one makes you happy, Patrick,' Xavier responded. 'I don't think there will be anyone left for you, but add another bullet to any that pleases you.'

After a few tense minutes, McGinnness and the sheriff reappeared, McGinness's face so deep red and angry that it looked like he could explode. 'Your story checks out,' Kittelson told Tom and the professor. 'Whenever you are in town, tell me how you wish to divide the reward and I will withdraw it from the bank. And I thank the Double Diamond for putting up the reward. It shows real public spiritedness.'

McGinness could have bitten through nails.

'And now,' Kittelson added, 'the matter of the titles of the horses you suggest rightfully belong to Double Diamond. Are those the animals in question?' he asked and pointed to the mares the professor had bought, which stood calmly watching over the top rail of the big corral as if they were theater-goers in their seats.

'Go to hell!' McGinness said harshly as he swung up on

his horse. 'There will be another day. Don't you doubt that!' he said to all, obviously including the sheriff.

Everyone was surprised to realize that Kittelson had his pistol drawn although pointed at no one. 'Yah. Now gentlemen, you seem a bit heated up. Ride out and don't turn back!'

'Another day,' McGinness repeated, his face red with fury. He snatched his horse's reins around and spurred it viciously. 'And what the hell am I paying you for?' they heard him snap at his riders.

Everyone watched the men until they had cleared the gap to the plains. 'And, now, perhaps Bridgette has some coffee,' Sheriff Kittelson said and went inside, followed by Xavier, the professor, and Tom. Patrick walked from the barn toward them.

'If anyone comes, have the fellow in the soddy fire a warning shot,' the professor told Tom and followed them into the house. Tom was obviously very surprised at this instruction but straightened his face before going inside.

CHAPTER TWENTY-FIVE

'You couldn't have pleased her any more with gold or silver!' the professor told Gaye as Rachel tossed crumbled up cornbread to the hens and rooster Gaye had brought to her. The professor and Gaye chuckled as Rachel directed Mose to make certain that the flat stone lying by the small opening into the back of the coop would close up tightly enough to keep varmints out of the chicken coop he had built from small aspen poles for her. 'She acts prouder than that red rooster,' the professor observed happily, as the rooster strutted around surveying its new kingdom.

'It's hard to imagine a happier woman,' Hattie said.

'As young and pretty as she is, she's also a very tough lady,' Doc said as he leaned by the wagon with his seemingly ever-present glass of whiskey. 'She took rough treatment both at the teacher house and outside Gaye's door,' he said. 'You would think she hadn't even stubbed her toe, no more effect than she shows.'

The memory of Rachel following the beating she took in the teacher house infuriated the professor all over again and made him even more appreciative of Mose's massive presence at the ranch whenever he and Xavier worked the gold seam or joined the Brights in scouring the surrounding plains for more mustangs to capture and add to their stock. Renaissance man was hardly the term the professor would have thought of when he first saw the massive man, but so far he had failed to find anything Mose couldn't do: shape iron into everything from hinges to horse shoes; handle the mares that had so recently run wild on the plains as if he'd raised them from their first days on earth; bake the finest scones and cookies he had ever tasted; and shoot equally well at targets as the professor and Xavier. They had also learned that he could read with the most finely accented British English. When questioned, Mose related his background: born a slave along the Georgia coast; sold as a youngster to an Englishman who ran a citrus and silk plantation along the Atlantic coast; freed to work as a sailor on the Englishman's sailing ships; and lived in Britain as servant and confidante to his former owner. The owner had noticed his ability to shape items and started him in training as a blacksmith and iron fabricator.

Eventually, Mose had emigrated to Indianola, Texas, and worked as an independent builder until a hurricane destroyed the city and took most of his accrued earnings. Like many he had moved to the frontier to seek his living.

CHAPTER TWENTY-SIX

'They're like a bunch of little boys getting set to go camping or fishing,' Hattie told Rachel as they watched the men making the last preparations for their latest venture.

Three large wagons were loaded, each with a pair of mules hitched to them, and a canvas cover pulled tightly over the body and tied down. A half dozen horses were tied to the back of the wagons by lead lines, and two saddled horses stood ready to leave. Mose's mule, Sweet Pea, stood unhitched and untied. Mose, the professor, Xavier, Angus Gillis, and Tom Bright bustled around checking the tie downs on the wagons, the saddles on the horses, and the weapons on their hips one more time. Ute squatted by Tarbaby, consoling him for being left behind to help guard the women.

Finally, Mose climbed up on his big wagon and took the reins, obviously ready to roll. The professor and Angus hugged and kissed their wives one more time. Xavier and Bridgette stepped around the corner of the house for their private leave-taking. The preacher and Patrick leaned against the house, Patrick obviously wishing he was accompanying the men traveling and the preacher just as obviously relieved that he wasn't. Rachel assured the professor one more time that the three women, Tarbaby, Patrick, and the preacher were more than a match for any trouble that might present itself and that the sheriff had promised to check regularly on them as well as the Brights' property. 'Go! Quit being such a worry-wart!' she told him, tiring of his lingering. 'We got a quilt to do while you're gone.'

Finally, the men were mounted on their horses or driving one of the wagons and rolled out. This expedition had begun when Ute had told the professor and Mose that they could do very well trading with the Utes to the North if Mose made arrow points, knife blades, and axe heads in his blacksmith shop. One foray with some of the items Mose made quickly but well resulted in acquiring two nice mares from trade as well as a couple of beautifully finished buffalo robes and a smattering of other furs. The professor, Xavier, Mose, and Angus, who, along with Hattie, were visiting, had been talking of the profits that could be made in such trade if only they could come up with suitable iron, especially noting how the metal rims of the wide-wheeled wagons commonly used for freight on the Plains was so easy to turn into the desired items.

'Damn plenty old wagon wheels out there,' Ute told them as he passed through.

'Where?' Angus asked.

'Up north,' he responded. When he saw how interested the men were, he continued. 'Three days' ride up the front of the mountains, way the hell back in canyons,' he said, then quickly looked to see if Rachel had heard. One of her main projects had become teaching Ute what words were swear words and discouraging him from using them. 'Fill Mose's big wagon three, four times,' he said.

'Do they belong to anyone?' Angus asked.

Ute shook his head. 'Horses, cows run loose there, too.'

Now, two weeks later, the men were on their way to hope-fully fill their wagons with scrap iron. Besides using it themselves, scrap iron would almost always be valuable in areas where freight service with the outside world was limited. There was also a good market for beef and horses at the time in Ft Sumner where the army was holding several thousand imprisoned Navajo. The men planned to divide the iron evenly, sell any cattle or horses they caught, and divide the money equally. Although the men realized the danger from attack if they were seen by the Double Diamond riders or by Comanches, who ranged to the edge of the Rockies, the atmosphere had taken on the mood of a recreational outing as they prepared. Once they were on their way, however, they settled down to business. Mose, Angus, and Tom drove the three wagons. Ute rode well ahead leading the way; Xavier and the professor swung well to either flank.

The men veered south to avoid the likelihood of bumping into Double Diamond riders and west until they were past the eastern face of the Sangre de Cristo Mountains and then northward for two more days. Already they had seen several bands of mustangs and several unbranded cattle that were up to four or five years of age and wild as buffalo. Rolling grassy plains stretched away to the horizon to the east, south, and north. The massive eastern face of the Rockies loomed only a few miles to the west. Water had been plentiful since streams ran from the mountains fairly often, many of them, the professor knew, soaking into the earth before traveling very far.

Looking ahead, the professor realized that he hadn't seen Ute for some time but wasn't concerned. Topping another rise, he saw a line of trees scattered ahead, an almost certain sign of a stream. As he watched this tree line,

Ute appeared over a rise and loped his horse toward the professor.

'Cross this stream, go into canyon,' Ute told him as he rode up. 'Everyone. . . .' he searched for words, motioned with his hands to come together.

'OK,' the professor replied and rode toward the wagons. Xavier had been watching the professor and Ute and turned to meet them at the wagons.

Everyone stopped in surprise at what they saw. Ten big wagons stood circled in the valley, at first glance as if they had stopped the night before as usual, but the silence and absence of people or livestock changed that perception. Grass and scattered brush had grown up around and under the wagons. Only tattered remnants of canvas survived of covers most wagons had probably had when they formed the circle some years earlier. Several horses and cattle scattered in the valley threw their heads up nervously and stared at these humans as if they were totally strange animals to them. After a while, first one, then two, and shortly all moved away toward the back of the canyon, all the while keeping watch of these new interlopers. Before long, all broke into a run into a side canyon off the main one.

'If that's a box canyon, we know where to hold the live-stock we catch,' Angus observed.

Mose's attention focused on the wagons. 'This beats a hen rooting,' he said. 'Whatever in the world happened?'

Ute shrugged his shoulders. 'None of my people know. My people and the Comanches stay away; figure the canyon is haunted.'

'Well you be right about one thing, Ute. We can fill these wagons with first-rate scrap metal,' Mose said. 'I'll take care of that and you fellows catch up some horses and cattle. We'll all be setting pretty when we get back.'

131

'If,' Xavier corrected. 'We better not count our chickens yet,' he said, 'as you Americans say.'

CHAPTER
TWENTY-SEVEN

' 'Tis me, Professor,' Bright announced. 'I'm alone.'

Everyone reappeared except Mose, the professor noticed. 'Smelled the coffee,' Bright said. He poured a cup and walked back into the darkness. Since the professor was to replace him as lookout soon, he refilled his coffee and moved away to join Bright where he had stopped by the horses tied to a stretched rope ready for emergency or night hawking.

'Something's out there,' Bright told the professor quietly. 'Don't know what or even how I know, but something's moving about.'

Hayes nodded. 'Know the feeling. And I was sitting there staring into the fire like a tenderfoot. If you'll make one more round, I'll take your place.'

'I'm out here, too, Professor.' Mose's voice drifted in, although the professor couldn't see any sign of him. Despite the moon not having risen, the stars made enough light to see somewhat. Finally, the professor saw the reflection of light from Mose's face. 'I'm not sleepy. I'm just going to ease out here and settle my soogins down in that little mesquite thicket for the night. You might wanta hum a little tune if you start to come nearby.' He chuckled softly.

Hayes returned to the fire and found the group still scattered about. Both Xavier and Angus faced away from the fire, readjusting their eyes to the darkness, the professor knew. 'Bright Boy says there's something moving about somewhere. We might better all scatter about just in case. Could be two-legged or four-legged varmints.' He walked away from the fire. Every person here, he knew, would account for themselves if anyone attacked.

The next morning, everyone was relieved to have had no trouble, but also certain that someone or something had prowled nearby; no tracks were found, a fact which made the professor more uneasy rather than reassured.

'Stock's got that canyon grazed down just about to nubbins,' Angus said as he poured coffee.

'I done got all the metal that's to be had,' Mose told them.

'What you say we round up what we can today and hit the trail tomorrow,' the professor asked.

'I say let's light a fucking shuck out of here, tomorrow,' Ute suggested. Others nodded their agreement.

The professor realized that he was going to have to speak to Ute about his language. Rachel would have a fit if the boy backslid that much in his language back home. *Home!* The professor realized how many years he had gone without having his own home to which he could return. And Rachel! He had wondered so many times if he would ever find a woman to partner with him like his fellow ranger, Arthur L. had found in Kathleen Painter. She had always welcomed A.J. home from his ranger ramblings warmly and sincerely, but the professor deeply missed the welcome from a woman of his own. He had wondered many times if he was capable of the kind of attachment he saw between his partner and Kathleen and often decided that there was something lacking in him that would prevent him from

133

finding that kind of bond. He was amazed every time he realized what a short time it had taken him to feel so deeply for Rachel. He often shook his head in wonder that he actually stepped out on to that depot landing toward Rachel as he had. Perhaps he should look Pitt up sometime and thank him for harassing Rachel. Somehow he couldn't imagine that he would have made the move he did if he hadn't been reacting against the bully and boor in Pitt. He laughed aloud at himself for thinking such; he didn't even notice that several of his cohorts on this venture were looking at him quizzically when he laughed aloud to himself. He did hear Mose laugh but didn't connect it to his own thoughts. *Life is good!* the professor thought as he felt warm inside and enjoyed the beauty of the morning sky coloring brightly in the east.

Mose and Ute were left with the camp while the others made sweeps gathering stock, either cattle or wild horses, already spotted and located. Ute walked to the fire and poured a cup of coffee. Mose gathered an armload of his tools to load into his wagon along with all the metal from the ruins of two very large abandoned wagons already packed away. In addition to loading up his tools and other supplies, he kept part of his attention up canyon where the horses, two mules, and cattle they had gathered grazed on the disappearing vegetation. With their camp and wagons in the narrowest neck of the canyon, the wild and semi-wild stock up canyon so far kept its distance. Steep canyon walls kept stock from getting out in any direction other than by the wagons and camp. The camp was set up right by the north edge of the canyon, almost directly under the steep walls. They had all agreed that today would be the last gather. After that they would brand all the new stock and head for home. Mose laid out the branding irons; each had brought one of their own irons. The professor asked Mose to make an iron for Ute, suggesting simply a U unless the youngster wished something else. 'And I don't see one for you, Mose. Be sure to make one for yourself as well. Should be pretty easy for you, with the wagon rod, tire rims, and what have you've salvaged.'

Mose stopped what he was doing and looked down at the ground for what seemed a long time. The professor busied himself for a moment then asked, 'What's wrong, Mose?'

'I ride for you,' Mose said.

'You ride *with* me, Mose,' the professor gently reminded him. 'And there's no reason for you not to have your own brand as well,' the professor responded. 'You can run your animals with ours or sell them or whatever you wish.'

'I never had a brand of my own,' Mose said.

'Well now you do, Mose. Now you do. And family, too, if you're willing to allow us the privilege of claiming you.'

'I'd like that, Professor, I sure would,' Mose finally said. After a moment, a crooked grin crinkled his face. 'Can I call you Papa?' Mose asked happily.

'Not if you want to remain family, Mose. Professor or A.J. will do.' The professor chuckled, and shook Mose's huge hand, almost intimidated as always when he felt the man's size and potential power.

Mose hummed as he worked while the other men rode away.

The first thing Mose noticed was Ute frozen motionless except for very slowly setting down his coffee cup as he stared toward the rock wall of the canyon. Mose followed his eyes and was startled to see three Apaches standing with rifles leveled toward him and Ute. He blinked twice trying to believe he was imagining the Apaches. No one could have approached from that way undetected, but they were there and very real. The Apaches wore moccasins extending well above the knee, a breechclout, a leather bandoleer

135

with rifle shells, a sheath and knife, a leather band holding their hair out of their faces and nothing else. Each held a rifle, all three Spencer repeaters, Mose noticed, holding them as if they were an extension of their bodies. Mose had never been so surprised, and then two more Apaches emerged, as if they were materializing out of thin air, dressed and armed the same way. He couldn't imagine five more dangerous-looking men. Their black eyes shone like polished stones; each man gave the impression that the desert had melted any kind of softness away, right down to bone, skin, stringy muscle, and sinew. Three had obvious bullet wound scars visible. Another had what looked like a knife scar down his left cheek. Only one had a few streaks of gray in his hair. Otherwise they could have been any age between twenty to fifty; their facial expressions looked as cold and dangerous as a coiled rattlesnake.

The warriors stood right beside the vertical wall of the canyon flanking the camp; no more than four or five feet separated one from the other, making Mose think that they must have approached up some minor ravine or unevenness his eyes couldn't detect. The one with streaks of gray took a couple of steps closer to the camp. Ute spoke in a language other than English and held his cup of coffee toward the warrior. The warrior looked at Ute for a moment and then, moving as quickly as any striking rattler slapped the coffee from Ute's hand with the muzzle of his Spencer. He continued to stare at first Ute and then at Mose, moving nothing but his eyes. 'Why Ute with black white man?' he asked in halting English.

Neither Ute nor Mose spoke. 'Hear black white man bleed red,' the Apache said and cocked his Spencer. He spoke in Apache to the others. Two of them aimed at Ute. 'Like wooly scalp,' the eldest warrior said, his English flat and expressionless.

Mose's mind ran desperately, searching for any possible chance to escape. He didn't take time to chastise himself for leaving his shotgun out of reach or for failing to wear his big Colt, which got in the way when handling and loading tools. Mose decided to make a move. Even if he didn't survive, he had to force the Apaches to fire their weapons. It almost certainly wouldn't save them, but gunshots would alert the others. Mose knew that he was quicker than almost anyone would expect from someone his size. He would make a slight feint to his left, dive hard right, then try to roll into the shallow ravine beside the wagon and grab his shotgun. Even if hit with the big slug from the Apache's Spencer, perhaps he could get into action with his shotgun.

The Apache standing nearest the steep canyon wall to Mose's left said something, sneering as he spoke, as if he was reading Mose's thoughts and taunting him. The warrior smiled malevolently and aimed his Spencer. Mose sensed movement atop the canyon wall.

Suddenly something dropped from the top of the canyon, a wriggling mass as it fell. Only when it landed on the warrior did Mose realize it was a rattlesnake. Now he could hear the rattling. The warrior flailed wildly to get the serpent off him. The other Apaches turned to look at the warrior as he yelled. The warrior with some gray hair suddenly bolted backwards. Without thinking, Mose dove for his shotgun. Ute dropped to the ground and rolled. The warriors all flailed and scrambled. The first warrior knocked the snake off him; it landed on the older warrior, who knocked it away with his rifle muzzle, right on to another.

They all scrambled, their enemies forgotten for a panicked moment. The two outer warriors slapped at the snake with their rifle muzzles until it fell away from the elder. When the snake was gone, the elder whirled back toward

Mose and Ute and found both holding their weapons leveled toward them. For what seemed a long time but was probably only seconds, the Apaches stared into the muzzles of Mose's Colt Revolving shotgun, ten-gauge bore, and Ute's rifle. The Apaches, veteran warriors, stood frozen, staring into what would be almost certain death if gunfire began. The warrior on the right flank seemed to be easing his hand on to his trigger like he was going to make a move. The sound of a rifle lever above caused them to look up from where the snake had dropped. Angus pointed his Henry Repeater toward them. The Apaches froze again. Mose spoke in Spanish; Ute spoke in another language. The eldest warrior said something sharply. The warrior hesitated but then moved his hand back away from the trigger. Suddenly, horses and cattle stampeded down the canyon toward the Apaches. Two were knocked down, winded. The professor and Bright Boy, swung their horses aside and pulled up with pistols leveled toward the Apaches. The standoff was obvious. Both sides would suffer bloody damage if battle commenced. Mose wasn't sure why gunfire didn't erupt, but it didn't.

Ute stood and spoke a few words and gestured in the sign language common on the Plains. Noise from the cliff drew the attention of all. On the other canyon wall opposite Angus stood Xavier, his rifle aimed at one of the warriors. The snake-bit Apache was the only person moving. He frantically tried to look over his shoulder to see the site of his snakebite. Ute lay his rifle down, picked up a buckskin pouch from the ground, and walked to the bitten warrior, swerving a couple of steps out of his way to pick up a burning stick from the fire. The bitten warrior pointed his rifle toward Ute as he approached. When close enough, Ute reached up and pushed the muzzle away from him but didn't attempt to take the weapon away. Instead, Ute took the warrior by the shoulder and turned him so that he could see his back. He pinched and prodded for at least a full minute, and then turned to the burning brand he had laid on a rock. The Apache flinched away, retreated a step, and pointed his muzzle back closer toward Ute but not directly against him. Ute ignored the warrior's actions, gathered some dried grass and twigs, sat them on the rock and fanned until he had a flame. He laid more twigs and small sticks into the fire and let it burn, the dried materials flaming up like tinder. Ute took out his knife and held the blade in the flames for a couple of minutes, and then fanned some of the smoke over himself; he took the warrior by the arm and pulled him over beside the fire and fanned smoke upon him as well. By now everyone in both groups watched as if mesmerized. Ute took his knife and mimed to the warrior that he was going to cut the wound. The Apache seemed torn between his distrust on one side and his desire to show contempt for the Ute. After a moment, he allowed Ute to continue but also drew his own knife from his scabbard and showed it to Ute in a somewhat threatening manner, the message clear.

Ute ignored the warrior's threat and made two cuts forming an 'x' over the bite. He fanned more smoke over the warrior, spit into his hands, took some ground herbs from his pouch, mixed them, and spread them over the cut. This done, he removed another smaller vial from his pouch, dipped his fingers into a black salve and rubbed it on to the cut. Ute passed the knife back through the smoke several times, wiped it on his pants and put it away. He began a chant, at the same time going through elaborate hand motions and facial expressions. After a couple of minutes, he halted, carefully inspected the bite again, and nodded as if approving what he saw. He faced the eldest warrior and went through a series of signs; the eldest warrior looked at the others and nodded. Several other warriors nodded slightly in apparent agreement. 'We go,' the eldest warrior told them. All turned and walked away. The bitten warrior was unsteady at first but seemed to fare better as he walked away.

A sharp whistle caught their attention. On the flat top, Angus had mounted his horse and signaled with his eyes toward the Apaches. He would see that they left.

'What did you tell them?' the professor asked.

'Told dumb shit dog-eating Apaches to go away. I had saved warrior from snake bite, but I wouldn't save any more. Told them to get the hell away and not to stop until they were in the warm springs of the Chiricahua Mountains.'

'And what did you do for the snake bite?'

'Snake fangs barely scratched dumb shit Apache. Probably no poison got in him. I cut the spot where they can't know that he wasn't really bitten. When no poison problem, they think I one heap big Ute medicine man. They don't want no more of me!'

'You know what I think?' the professor asked.

'That it's time we got our bohunkuses back home?' Mose asked.

'Exactly!' Xavier chimed in.

In an hour, the wagons were loaded, the horses and cattle herded out of the canyon, and the greatly enlarged caravan headed back toward home. The men's spirits were suddenly as high as they had been on leaving home a few days earlier.

CHAPTER
TWENTY-EIGHT

Preacher Tolliver wiped his face from sweat once again; although the air was very cool even in the sun, it was much less so in the shade beneath the leaning stone outcrop where the three men worked. Fear so strong that it almost made the preacher physically ill wracked him each time he worked extracting gold from the rock, and yet, while he belly-ached constantly about the danger, he never missed his turn in the most dangerous spot and was even developing rather good skill at removing as much gold as possible while removing no more stone than necessary. Although they seldom voiced it aloud, all three felt that the stone seemed to be tilting even more sharply than before, but they were extracting the richest ore yet. He climbed the ladder to the cut they were currently working about as eagerly as a condemned man would climb the gallows steps. He leaned outward, placed his bit into the hole he had been drilling, and slammed it with his single jack. Metal clanged on metal; the rock seemed to groan. One more inch, and he would take a chisel and attempt to pry out some of the 'jewelry rock' they were extracting today. Thunder rumbled in the distance; lightning flashed more closely. The preacher yelled, grabbed for the ladder sides but fell backwards; his body yanked violently as his leg slid forward between the ladder rungs and caught. He screamed in pain.

The professor and Xavier sprinted to the ladder. Xavier

caught the preacher's shoulders, first steadied him, and then lifted to relieve some of the pressure on the leg caught in the ladder. The professor scrambled up several rungs of the ladder, hooked one arm through it, grasped the preacher's leg, and almost dropped him. He looked below at Xavier, shook his head but lifted it again. The preacher screamed again, and then, mercifully, passed out. The two combined to remove the preacher from the ladder and carry him well beyond the stone shaft before placing him gently on the ground.

The professor took his knife from his pocket and sliced the leg of the preacher's pants on first one side then the other, all the way to the upper thigh. The leg hardly looked human. Several bends meant that the bone had broken in multiple places; the flesh was already darkening with interior bleeding. The professor stood, cupped his hands around his mouth and called, 'Ute! Ute!' Almost immediately the boy's head popped over the side of a boulder down the ridge. 'Get Mose and the wagon!' the professor called out. 'Quickly!'

'Let's hope he stays unconscious,' Xavier said.

The professor hurried to his horse. 'We need splints,' he told Xavier and rode away. He thought he heard the wagon although he knew Ute could not have gotten to the cabin in so short a time. But to his surprise, the wagon barreled in sight just as he started back into his saddle with limbs quickly cut from the nearest tree, Mose driving so fast that Rachel's hair streamed behind her as she held on to the wagon seat beneath her with one hand and dug into the bag in the wagon beside her. Suddenly she lurched to the side as Mose turned the team of mules sharply to his left to approach the mining site. Without looking, Mose reached with his huge right hand, grabbed Rachel by the arm, steadied her, and continued up the hill without looking away from his path.

'Splints!' the professor yelled and held tree limbs aloft as he rode toward where the preacher lay. Mose, Rachel, and the wagon skidded to a stop near them. The big black mules stamped and tossed their heads excitedly but stood in place as Mose quickly knotted the reins to the frame of the wagon seat. Rachel nodded understanding and turned to dig into a large bag she had brought, quickly pulling out rolled strips of cloth. The three of them arrived at the same time and immediately gathered beside the preacher. 'Lord God above!' Mose proclaimed as he looked at the mining site, which he'd not seen before. 'Lord have mercy!' he added quietly when he looked at the preacher.

Mose pulled his belt knife and cut the two halves of the preacher's pants legs and quickly tore both into strips. He took the splints from the professor's hands and placed them along the preacher's legs, looked carefully and re-positioned them slightly. 'Hold these in place, Miss Rachel,' he said. Once she had them, he tied strips to hold the splints in place while he worked, and then snugly wrapped and tied them. No one spoke the whole time Mose worked. 'You hold his leg real steady,' he told Xavier as he placed his arms underneath the preacher and lifted him as easily and gently as one would lift a newborn. 'Y'all pray that the preacher stays out until we get him to town.'

The professor quickly laid out a blanket roll Rachel had grabbed as Mose climbed into the wagon. Mose laid the preacher down gently. 'It might be better to bring Doc to the cabin,' Xavier said. 'The ride might kill him.'

'No, suh,' Mose said quietly but confidently. 'The preacher is going to need to be in town with the doctor, and it's better to drive him there while he's passed out.'

The professor thought a moment. 'All right. Xavier, you and Ute stay here and keep your eyes open. Forget every-thing except guarding this valley,' he said.

'There's a Bible in the house,' Mose told Xavier and Ute. 'I think you best be reading it and praying while we're gone.' Mose took the reins as the professor climbed into the back with Rachel and the preacher. The preacher groaned with pain, despite being unconscious, as the wagon rolled and turned to descend the hill and begin the drive toward town. Ute tossed the professor's rifle to him.

'Professor,' Mose said. 'Ahead.'

The professor looked up. Five men sat their horses spaced across the road facing them. 'What do you think?' he asked.

'There are at least two more in the rocks to our right,' Rachel responded, although he had meant to be asking Mose. 'If we stop, I think they will kill us,' she added.

The professor looked sharply at her, surprised that she could say that so analytically and dispassionately. He agreed, of course. 'Mose?' he asked.

'These two mules can really stretch out and get it, Professor. I figure our chances are better with our mules running than us sitting still, shooting it out,' Mose answered.

'Get down on the floor right against the front, Rachel,' the professor told her.

'But I can—' she objected.

'You can help most by not making Mose or me worry about you,' he told her firmly but calmly.

She did as he suggested. The professor took one of his pistols from his waistband and handed it to her, and then a handful of cartridges. She checked the pistol, slid a cartridge into the empty chamber on which his hammer normally rested, and dropped the other cartridges into a deep pocket on her dress. 'If they get close, they won't expect shots from you, lying in the wagon bed,' he told her.

'If it comes to that, aim for the middle of their body or even at their horse,' he told her.

'Your judgment on when to whip them up, Mose,' the professor said, calmly. 'I presume you do have that blunderbuss of yours?'

'I got my britches on, you know I got my shotgun,' he chuckled. 'I wish we had Sweet Pea and Tarbaby with us,' he added. 'They'd purely love this upscuddle.' Mose reached into the wagon bottom by his foot and sat his shotgun up, muzzle down, the stock leaning against his leg and the seat. 'Just a little closer,' he said.

Mose and Rachel were both shocked to see the professor raise his hands into the air as if surrendering. 'A.J., we can't surrender to them!' Rachel scolded.

'Slow down just a little, right before you slap it to the mules,' the professor said. 'Maybe we can surprise them a little.'

Mose made a show of drawing back on the reins, although he was actually only taking up slack, not reining back. The riders started forward toward the wagon. Mose screamed like a catamount with his tail on fire and, at the same moment, slapped the mules hard with the reins. The big, long-legged mules jumped like Moses had stuck hot coals under their tails.

The riders yanked on their reins in surprise for a moment before they spurred their horses toward the wagon. Mose lifted his shotgun, gripping it in his right hand like it was a pistol, and blasted two quick shots, emptying two saddles.

The professor lifted his rifle and began firing rapidly. He knocked one rider to the ground and burned another rider's horse, setting off a fit of bucking that left the rider holding desperately to the horse's neck and his saddle-horn trying to stay aboard. The wagon hit a bump so severe that

145

the wagon bounced into the air. The professor felt himself lifted into the air for a moment. Rachel grabbed the preacher to try to hold him in place, but he screamed when the wagon struck the ground again. The fifth rider turned his horse and raced away from the wagon, while a new rider raced toward the wagon from each side. Rachel popped up, grabbed Mose's shotgun where he had set it back down and was lashing the mules, and placed it back against him. The surprise at being so treated by the usually gentle Mose had caused the mules to jolt into a speed beyond what even they could normally run.

The professor aimed the best he could with the wagon now bouncing along like a runaway, lowered his sights and squeezed off another shot. The horse carrying the closer of the two approaching riders collapsed forward; the rider flew through the air, hit, rolled several somersaults, and lay still. The professor ducked when Rachel turned and pointed her pistol to the opposite side. She fired three quick shots; the second of the two charging riders' horses fell sideways and rolled over its rider.

The professor raised his muzzle and fired three quick shots toward the one rider left and now racing away. He knew the odds of hitting him or his horse were slim, but wanted to send him on his way, and was rewarded when his horse jumped and sunfished, almost dumping his rider before straightening out.

Loud groans came from behind the professor. He whirled, terrified, and felt somewhat guilty when he realized how relieved he was to see that it was the preacher who was groaning in agony from the wild bouncing the wagon had done while the firefight went on, rather than Rachel, as he had feared; he realized how lost he would be if Rachel was wounded or worse.

Gradually, Mose managed to regain control over the

mules and pulled them down to a stop. Rachel worked over the preacher although she couldn't do much more than pamper him; he moaned his agony despite being only partially conscious. 'The splints seem to have held,' Rachel told the professor and Mose after checking him over thoroughly.

A look of terrible shock followed by abject terror on Mose's face caused the professor to stop breathing. He followed his eyes and saw blood beginning to soak through the shoulder of Rachel's dress. Her face showed as much surprise as the professor. She followed their eyes and noticed the blood on her shoulder for the first time. She calmly lifted the neck of her dress to where she could see underneath the bloody cloth, showing no more concern than if treating a splinter or thorn. 'Let me see your handkerchief,' she told the professor. 'It's just a scratch. I didn't even feel it.'

Almost in a daze, the professor handed Rachel his handkerchief. She calmly placed it over the scratch, where it was held in place by her dress, and then turned back to the preacher. 'I think we need to get him to the doctor,' she told them, and paid no further attention to her bloody shoulder.

'Lord, Miss Rachel!' Mose said quietly but with emotion, and started the mules toward town.

CHAPTER TWENTY-NINE

'I love fried fish,' Rachel enthused. 'I've seen several really nice trout in this pool!'

Rachel rode her roan mare, a picnic basket tied behind her saddle, a fishing pole in her left hand. Mose rode slightly behind her, silent but his disapproval obvious in his every fiber. Rachel managed to ignore it.

The professor and Xavier had left before daylight riding to scout a band of wild horses they had noticed recently ranging on the other side of San Juan. Ute had left the previous day with several dozen arrow heads, some knife blades, and some other items Mose had cut and shaped from the iron rim taken from the burned out wagons they had found. Mose and the professor had agreed that Ute could place any mares he acquired trading with the Utes on the ranch to breed with Red and begin his own string of horses. Ute also had wages the professor had paid him and had talked of what trade items he would buy in town to add to his iron arrow heads and knife blades. Everyone else on the ranch had become quite amused at Ute's enthusiasm and privately made comments about their 'budding entrepreneur'. He had awakened and departed even before the professor and Xavier. The preacher remained in town receiving treatment from the doctor.

Mose obviously didn't share Rachel's enthusiasm for this outing as he rode his huge, ugly mule, a fishing pole sticking underneath the skirt of his saddle, his shotgun in his saddle scabbard, his eyes scanning the rim rock above the canyon that led from their valley to the open plains beyond. 'I just don't know, Missy,' he protested for the third time in the half mile after they left their valley. 'Don't know why, but my scalp is itching just like it used to when I was near Comanches down in Texas.'

'There are no Comanches here,' Rachel assured him playfully.

'No'm,' he complained, 'but there's them white renegades worser'n any redskin.'

'Speak proper English, Mose,' Rachel chided him. She hated it when he lapsed into dialect, what she referred to as his 'shuffle your feet' mode.

'Why yes, indeed, Mrs Hayes,' Mose said irritably in the very proper British English Rachel had discovered he could speak, what he referred to as his 'butler' English. 'I must say, I hope that you remembered our tea and crumpets. I wish I'd had time to pack some blood pudding and chips to go with our fi—'

A rifle cracked; Mose flew backwards out of his saddle. Sweet Pea whirled and raced back up the canyon, dragging Mose with his foot caught in the stirrup and flopping lifelessly, his presence terrifying the excitable mule, and Tarbaby racing along behind. 'Mose!' Rachel cried. She spurred her horse to pursue, but, almost immediately, heard a second rifle shot; her mare broke stride, reared on her back legs, and fell backwards. Sudden pain seared Rachel but quickly disappeared into darkness. The mare kicked several times then grew still, blood flowing from a hole behind its left ear.

'I hope the hell she's not dead,' the tallest of three riders said as they emerged from a nest of rocks on the side of the canyon. 'She won't do us much good if she's dead.'

'Hell! Perfesser won't know if she's dead or not,' another responded. 'It ain't like we're going to let him and that Frenchie ride away alive, no how.'

'She'd be more fun alive,' the third added, as he dug a small canvas bag and red bandanna out of his saddle-bag. 'This oughta be a good place,' he said as he tied the bag around a small cottonwood tree and the red bandanna beside it.

The three tied Rachel across the front of one of their saddles and rode away.

CHAPTER THIRTY

The professor and Xavier turned their horses into the canyon leading to their valley, talking enthusiastically about the wild horses they had gotten a good look at after seeing them only seen fleetingly in the past. Xavier held his hand out to halt the professor. 'A.J.' he said quietly.

The professor spotted the red bandanna and white bag tied to the tree ahead. Both sat their horses and carefully scanned the canyon and rim rock above, looking for any signs of anyone hiding. 'Why would they have put out a red flag if they wanted to dry gulch us?' Xavier asked.

'I'll go to the tree; you stay back here and cover me,' the professor told Xavier, drawing his rifle and spurring his horse forward.

Xavier also drew his rifle and scanned the area carefully, turning his horse in a complete circle doing while so. Nothing moved. A meadow lark sang; a mourning dove in the distance called its lonesome call. A mule deer stood by the creek watching the professor. Nothing except the red flag seemed out of the ordinary. As he saw the professor take the bag down, he felt almost like he'd been punched in the belly. Well beyond the professor, he noticed the tracks of several horses coming in their direction. In the bend of the canyon ahead, he could see a tiny portion of what he decided was Rachel's mare, lying on the ground. He spurred his horse forward beside the professor.

'Rachel,' the professor gasped, looking at a sheet of paper. Xavier had never seen the professor look so stricken.

Xavier felt a sickness in the pit of his stomach.

'A.J.,' was all he managed to say, and point toward what he was now pretty sure was her mare.

'Damn!' the professor said, the first time Xavier had ever heard him use profanity.

Xavier reached out and grasped the reins to the mustang mare the professor was riding. The professor started to spur the horse, but turned fiercely toward Xavier.

'If Rachel is caught or taken, she needs us alive and alert,' Xavier said. 'You go straight ahead; I'll swing up the other side of the canyon.'

'They have Rachel,' the professor said, lifting the message toward Xavier. 'They say she's alive and unhurt. I'm to write a bill of sale transferring ownership of the land to them. Meet them at sunset in Bunko Canyon.'

Xavier thought quietly a moment. 'Still need to be careful. Could be a lie,' he said.

The professor nodded numbly and started his horse forward. A couple of minutes later, he arrived at what turned out to be Rachel's mare, while Xavier circled more widely. Xavier joined the professor a couple of minutes later. The professor stared into space, the expression on his face terrible to see. Xavier shivered at the sight despite all the battles he had experienced in his lifetime. Both sat silently for what seemed a long time. 'There's no blood, here, other than from the mare,' Xavier finally pointed out.

The professor nodded, but pointed ahead. Xavier followed the line of his finger and saw a red patch on the ground. He inhaled sharply, but controlled himself and cut his eyes to the professor. The professor rode his horse forward. Xavier again swung wider rather than take the direct route, which would have placed the two in a position that would make both of them vulnerable to a single gunman.

The professor was already on the ground when Xavier arrived. A large splotch of blood stained the ground; the sod was torn. It was obvious that a large mule, undoubtedly Sweet Pea, Xavier figured, had whirled and raced away. He could see a couple more spots of blood ahead. He wished he was much better at reading tracks and sign. He and the professor had laughed just a few hours before at how poorly both of them tracked and read sign compared to many westerners. He saw no humor now at their shortcoming. It did look, however, like Mose had been shot from his mule, caught his foot in a stirrup, and been dragged away as the mule raced toward its barn.

'Let's bust it to the cabin,' Xavier suggested. 'If anyone's looking for us, we can't sneak up on them, but maybe we can make them miss if we ride in fast as we can.'

The professor jabbed his spurs into his mount's side. The mare, which had run wild only a couple of months ago, leapt into action, racing up the canyon. A count behind, Xavier did the same. They raced side by through the canyon toward the cabin, lying low on the necks of their mounts. Sweet Pea stood outside the barn door, Mose, obviously unconscious, beside it on the ground, his left foot still hanging in the stirrup. Xavier jumped off his horse and burst into the cabin, his rifle in his hands. The professor danced his horse looking around for any signs of ambush.

'Empty,' Xavier said as he emerged back through the cabin door.

'No one out here . . . so far,' the professor said.

Xavier was relieved to see that the professor was back into his warrior mode, coolly surveying the scene. 'I'll approach the mule. You get your lasso ready in case. No telling what this mule will do.' From day one, everyone had taken the attitude that only Mose dealt with Sweet Pea. Even when one approached casually in the mule's general direction, she bared her teeth, laid her ears back, and either blew like a snake or rumbled deeply in her chest like a threatening grizzly bear. Tarbaby sat with her body touching Mose; she whined and looked pitifully toward the professor in stark contrast to her usual aggressiveness.

The professor stuck his rifle back into his saddle scabbard, drew his pistol and carefully approached the mule, which turned a big eye toward him. 'Easy, Sweet Pea,' he purred, and kept sweet-talking her. He was shocked that Sweet Pea didn't bare her teeth, lay her ears back, dance away, or threaten to kick him. She could have just as easily been a lady's Sunday afternoon mare awaiting a sugar cube. The professor holstered his pistol. 'Keep a bead on her head,' he told Xavier. 'If she goes beserk, shoot her so we can get Mose loose.'

'OK,' Xavier answered tensely.

The professor squatted by Mose and placed his fingers on the big man's neck. 'He's alive,' he told Xavier. He took Mose's foot with one hand and the stirrup with the other. 'Back,' the professor said before he realized how unlikely it was that the big mule would do anything unless Mose ordered her. But to the professor's shock, Sweet Pea backed and stopped immediately when the professor told her to whoa. He stood and led Sweet Pea to a hitch post outside the barn, the usually fierce animal leading as easily as any pet, never taking her eyes off Mose.

'He's been shot,' Xavier told the professor when he turned away from Sweet Pea. 'If this is the only gunshot, he was just knocked out by the fall and being dragged.'

Professor Hayes took his canteen from his own saddle, wet his bandanna, and began bathing Mose's face. Mose groaned and turned his head side to side. The professor poured water gently over Mose's face and patted his cheeks. The big man popped his eyes open, looked around for a moment as if puzzled, then jerked, and tried to sit up. 'Miz Rachel!' he said.

The professor held Mose in place and put the canteen to his lips. 'She's been taken by the Double Diamond,' he told her.

The big man's eyes were alert almost immediately; he tried again and managed to sit up. 'I can track better than either of you,' he said. 'Get me up on Sweet Pea!'

'They left a note,' the professor told him. 'We're to meet them at sundown. We need to plan. And we won't have to track.'

CHAPTER THIRTY-ONE

'I wish we had time to get the Bright boys to help us,' Xavier said as he, the professor, and Mose rode into Bunco Canyon.

'No time,' the professor said. For what seemed like the hundredth time, he glanced at Mose to reassure himself that the big man was still upright in his saddle.

Mose saw his concern and told him, 'I'll be here when this shindig is over, Professor. We gonna make them pay for hurting Miss Rachel.' Tarbaby trotted beside Sweet Pea and watched Mose as anxiously as did the professor.

'Remember, I'll do the talking,' the professor told his companions. 'Only one person needs to negotiate with them. I want to establish that Rachel is alive before I give them this deed.' The fact that the professor was repeating the same thing for the fourth time told Xavier how nervous he, normally one of the coolest men he had ever seen in a crisis, was as they approached the canyon.

Bunco canyon didn't resemble those occupied by the professor, the Brights, and the Gillises. Bunco was really a shallow valley of ten acres or less, rimmed by sloping sides with large rock outcroppings, but not the sheer walls of those canyons which cut into the Mesa. Two copses of pinon darkened the sides. Short brown grass covered the valley. A few willows and a large cottonwood marked the site of the one small spring in the valley.

'There they are,' Mose said, as seven riders approached from behind large rocks near the valley top. Pitt Randall was immediately obvious due to his size and the white stallion he frequently rode. The professor placed the man riding to Pitt's right as the foreman of the Double Diamond.

'Rachel's not with them,' he said.

'We need to know where she is,' Xavier said. 'You know they're not going to let any of us ride out of here?' he added.

'They got us in a bind,' the professor agreed. 'If we can't work out a trade, we'll have to kill all of them and hope that whoever has Rachel won't actually kill a woman in cold blood.'

The seven riders drew up facing the professor, Xavier, and Mose. The foreman let his surprise show when he saw Mose sitting straight in his saddle. In his mind, the professor marked him as the probable shooter of Rachel's horse and Mose. The professor had, during his ranger years, faced shootouts on multiple occasions, but he hadn't been worried about Rachel in those cases.

'That the deed?' Pitt asked the professor, nodding toward the paper folded in his shirt pocket. When the professor sat silently staring at him, Pitt grinned and leaned comfortably forward with both hands on his saddle-horn. 'I don't like the look in your eyes,' he told the professor. 'Don't be stupid. All I have to do is lift my hand and our guy blasts Mrs Hayes with a shotgun.'

'You lift even one finger off that saddle-horn, and you're a dead man,' Hayes told Pitt quietly. The professor's face didn't change at the threat, but, underneath his confident expression, his mind was racing for some chance – any chance – to get Rachel away without her being harmed.

Pitt's face darkened; his face showed anger but also concern. 'One shot and she dies,' Pitt warned.

'I don't think it will do you any good, dead, yourself,' the professor replied. 'I always figured you were behind all of this.'

'But not only me,' Pitt grinned.

'A.J.!' Rachel's voice called out at that moment. 'I'm free of them. Do what you need to do.'

The faces of all the Double Diamond gunmen showed surprise. 'She's lying!' the foreman sputtered. 'She's under the gun.'

A high-pitched war whoop floated down from the ridge. 'Don't worry about the fat sumbitch on the end! Ute has him!' The voice was obviously that of Ute.

At that point another very large rider approached from the side, a direction from which none of the others had come. Pitt Randall smiled. 'Don't worry about the woman, then, Professor. Just worry about eight guns now against you.' He nodded his head toward Devlon as he approached them. 'Eight against three.'

The professor noticed Xavier turn his horse about forty-five degrees to his left so that he faced more toward Devlon but still had a couple of the gunmen in his sight.

But when Devlon reached them, he turned his horse toward Pitt rather than Xavier and the professor. 'Seven against four, Pitt,' Devlon said. 'I told you from the start that I wasn't with you on this. I'm ashamed every day that I partnered with you in the bordello, but, like I've told you from the beginning, I'm not a thief. And I'm certainly not a killer or abuser of decent women.'

Pitt's face fell, and then turned furious. 'You double-dealing . . .' he sputtered at a loss for words.

'Professor!' another voice called from the ridge. 'I think you called me the sodhouse shooter. I got my rifle on the one on the end, west side.'

A young gunman next to the end chuckled and tossed his shoulder-length yellow hair back and forth, finally staring at Mose. 'You'll still die,' he said. 'You don't think this nigger will stand, do you? And I can get three of you before you clear leather.'

Mose stared at the young man for a moment, and then pointed toward him. 'Tarbaby. That one.' The huge black dog growled very deep in his chest, his eyes locked on the gunman. Mose lapsed into his butler English. 'I say, chaps. Are we going to shoot or just sit and—' The gunmen's eyes jerked toward Mose in surprise.

'Sic him!' Mose snapped. Tarbaby instantly flashed toward the young gunman. Mose fired his big shotgun at the next gunman. The gunman flew backwards out of his saddle even before his hand moved toward his pistol.

Two rifle shots followed almost immediately from the ridge. Two more Double-Diamond gunmen fell from their saddles. The professor whipped both of his Navy Colts from his waistband and blasted the foreman just as the foreman shot. The foreman fell from his saddle. The professor heard another shotgun blast, this one from the trees to their left. 'Rachel. . . !' he began, but slid from his saddle to the ground. On the way down, he saw Pitt draw rapidly and fire. Devlon jerked sidewards to his left, but continued his

157

draw as he slowly twisted from his saddle. Pitt began a pivot to his right to bring his pistol in line with Xavier, but Devlon's pistol fired before Pitt could aim and fire again. Pitt froze for a moment and fell from his saddle, a single hole in his forehead. As Pitt fell, Devlon turned limp and fell from his saddle, smoke drifting from his pistol. Xavier fired three times into the Double Diamond gunman facing him.

The professor hit the ground, weak, for whatever reason he wasn't certain. The scene blurred. He shook his head several times; the scene cleared but he still felt weak. The silence was as startling as the gunshots had been. All of the Double Diamond gunmen were on the ground as were he and Devlon, he saw, as he scanned the scene. A woman rode wildly toward them, like a Texas Comanche, he thought. Ute followed about ten yards behind. She certainly looked unharmed, the way she rode.

From his left, he saw another rider coming, riding a mule. Things blurred again. Through the blur, he saw an unfamiliar face to his right, attached to a small light-skinned man with long red hair sticking out from his hat. The professor patted the ground trying to find his pistol, but noticed that the man slid his rifle into his saddle scabbard on a black mare, a black mare with the Brights' brand, he noticed.

The next thing the professor knew, he woke enmeshed in long arms, long arms with full-length sleeves, strong hands and soft breasts.

'Rachel!' He quickly looked her over from feet to hair to see that she was unhurt. 'God! You're beautiful!' he exclaimed. He grabbed her to hug her even more tightly, but his left arm didn't work. He noticed blood smeared on her dress. 'You're shot!' he told her.

'No, you're shot,' a male voice answered. The professor

smelled whiskey. He recognized Doc, holding, as always, his glass, or in this case, a metal cup, of whiskey. 'For you,' Doc told him.

'Where'd you come from?' the professor asked.

'The Swede brought me.'

'Yah! I figured someone had a leak or two to plug,' Sheriff Kittelson told him.

'Devlon?' the professor asked.

'Like you,' Doc said. 'Leaking a little but OK. And soaking up my whiskey.' He pointed and the professor saw Devlon sitting up, a bloody patch on his shirt, which had been cut away and a bandage applied. He looked down and saw a bandage on his own shoulder. 'The two of you were hit about the same place,' he told the professor, 'but he doesn't have the tender care you're going to get.'

The professor looked to the other side and saw the sheriff talking to a stranger. When they saw the professor noticing them, they walked up to him. 'I believe you called me the soddy shooter,' the stranger said, offering his hand for a shake.

Sheriff Kittelson looked at the soddy shooter as if deep in thought. 'Be dad-gummed if this fellow doesn't look familiar,' the sheriff mused, but smiled. 'But I went through all my wanted notices just this week, and there wasn't a single person whose name started with an S, neither Soddy nor Shooter, so this fellow is welcome here.' He smiled widely, pulled his pants up over his buttocks and turned away.

Doc stopped by the professor and Rachel again. He held out his whiskey cup. 'Drink some more of this,' he said. 'Danged if I ever treated three fellows at once with such similar wounds. You, Mose, and Devlon are hit in almost the identical spot in the left shoulder. Bullets missed bones by less than an inch in all three.'

'I heard a shot to our left right after the fight, a shotgun blast,' the professor told Doc.

'Yep. Swede's old shotgun. One of these Double Diamond boys was drawing a bead on one of you when we saw him. Swede might look slow, but he shot from the hip, like a quail was flushing wild from a briar patch and ended that outlaw.'

Ute rode up just as Doc turned away. He was riding a gray mare that the professor had never seen. On separate leads, he had four other mares, each clean-limbed and strong-looking. Ute pointed proudly. 'I was coming back with these horses I traded for, saw the outlaws,' he said, obviously as proud of his trading as of helping take down the Double Diamond riders.

'Tarbaby did right good, didn't he, Professor?' Mose asked.

'He did way better than right good,' the professor told Mose. 'And you did, too. I think we wouldn't have made it out of this fight if you and Tarbaby hadn't surprised them. I'm very happy to have you as part of our family,' he told Mose, as Rachel joined them. She hugged the big man. The professor would have almost sworn that he could see Mose blush, despite his very dark complexion.

'Speaking of home,' Rachel said, 'I believe you and Mose can ride. And A.J., I want that damn gold trap blasted down this week! I came out here for a home, not a gold mine!'

'Yes ma'am,' the professor told her as they rode toward home.